Alex reached out and handed her a horse blanket, which Cassandra wrapped around herself. In its meager, though welcome, warmth, she made herself as comfortable as possible. Alex knelt down and gathered her into strong arms. The two women were silent.
"I am beginning to feel warm again," Cassandra said after a while. Her mouth was near Alex's neck. She burrowed deeper into Alex's arms. Cassandra breathed in the musky odor of sweat and horse and rain and somehow it did not offend her. She knew that she, too, must smell of horse and wet earth. Cassandra made a soft sound and found herself looking into Alex's golden-brown eyes. Her lips parted involuntarily, and, with a groan, Alex placed her mouth on Cassie's.
Alex unbuttoned Cassie's long-sleeved jacket. Her work-roughened hands caressed Cassie's breasts . . .

ABOUT THE AUTHOR

Barbara Johnson lives in a Maryland suburb with her lover of eighteen years, *WordGaymes* creator Kathleen DeBold, where she creates fantasies to counteract daily life editing NASA computer manuals. An animal lover, she also lives with three cats (Rita Mae, Isis, and Bruce) and three birds (Paco, Oscar, and Bosie), who control her life. Besides writing, her hobbies include reading, traveling, going to the ballet, and collecting snails (not the real ones).

Stonehurst

BY BARBARA JOHNSON

The Naiad Press, Inc.
1992

Copyright © 1992 by Barbara Johnson

All rights reserved. No part of this book may be reproduced or transmitted in any form or by any means, electronic or mechanical, including photocopying, without permission in writing from the publisher.

Printed in the United States of America on acid-free paper
First Edition

Edited by Christine Cassidy
Cover design by Pat Tong and Bonnie Liss
　(Phoenix Graphics)
Typeset by Sandi Stancil

Library of Congress Cataloging-in-Publication Data

Johnson, Barbara, 1955 —
　Stonehurst / by Barbara Johnson.
　　p.　　cm.
　ISBN 1-56280-024-8 : $9.95
　I. Title.
PS3560.037174S76　　1992
813'.54—dc20　　　　　　　　　　　　　　　　　92-18630
　　　　　　　　　　　　　　　　　　　　　　　　CIP

Dedicated to

*Kathy Marino
(1959–1986)*

ACKNOWLEDGMENTS

Many thanks to Barbara Grier for making my dream come true and to my editor, Christine Cassidy, for her wonderful suggestions. Special thanks to my lover Kathleen, for her patience; her gentle, yet persistent, nagging; and her excellent advice during the long process of writing *Stonehurst*. To all my friends, too numerous to name, thank you for your support and encouragement. And a very heartfelt thanks to Loretta and Cathryn, two of the best personal publicity agents a new writer could ever hope for.

CHAPTER 1

With a swish of her crimson velvet riding skirt, eighteen-year-old Lady Cassandra Stonehurst stopped in open-mouthed astonishment. There before her, mucking out Appleton's stable was, unmistakably, a woman. The dark chestnut hair was cropped short; the snug, tan breeches and tight, stained brown boots showed off well-muscled thighs and calves. The loose white shirt, however, could not hide the swell of softly rounded breasts swaying gently with each movement of the woman's task. Mesmerized, Lady

Cassandra watched the fluid movements for some minutes before coughing discreetly. She blushed at the impropriety of the woman's attire. No properly brought up female would flaunt herself so brazenly, servant or no.

The woman turned slowly, raising an eyebrow. Lady Cassandra stood speechless. Quickly touching two fingers from her right hand to her forehead, the woman bowed her head in deference. The action brought Cassandra out of her trance. She impatiently struck her riding whip against her skirt.

"Where is Appleton?" she demanded. "He should have been brought to the house already. I do not appreciate having to come down to the stables myself. Please saddle him up immediately."

"Yes, Lady Cassandra," the woman said with a trace of insolence. She dropped the rake and headed toward the opposite end of the stable where Appleton was temporarily tethered.

The stablemaid walked confidently and with purpose, her rounded hips accentuated by the snug breeches. Instinctively aware that the woman resented showing subservience, Cassandra wondered about this servant's family background. She watched as the woman expertly saddled the high-spirited stallion, who was eager for a gallop over the gently rolling hills and wooded grounds of the Stonehurst family estate. Again, she felt herself blushing as the woman brought the stallion forward to the mounting block. The stablemaid's clothing left nothing to the imagination.

Cassandra took the woman's tanned, calloused hand and hoisted herself onto the awkward sidesaddle, sucking in her breath at the tremor caused by the woman's touch. Flustered, she refused to look at her as she settled onto the saddle. To hide her discomfort and embarrassment, Cassandra spoke in a tone more haughty than she intended.

"What is your name, young woman?"

The woman smirked slightly, but answered with the proper deference. "Alex, milady."

"Alex? Alex is no proper name for a gently bred woman," Cassandra said. Appleton impatiently stamped his hooves.

"But I am no gently bred woman, milady. Am I?"

Cassandra ignored the insolence of the reply. She spurred her horse and cantered away. She was unaccompanied, her parents having long ago given up forcing her to take a groom along as an escort. Grooms were a hindrance, Cassandra had argued, and besides, she felt perfectly safe on her own. Her parents knew she would only send a groom back after the first mile anyway.

Cassandra decided she must speak to James, the head groom, about the cheeky young woman working in his stable. Her papa would surely disapprove of a girl working a man's job and dressed in men's clothing, but she was inexplicably reluctant to say something to him. Could it be that she was secretly, pleasantly scandalized to see Alex in those form-fitting breeches that hugged her body so disgracefully? The only woman whose body Cassandra saw so exposed was her own when she bathed. She shook her head to rid herself of improper thoughts and urged Appleton into an almost-reckless gallop.

* * * * *

From the stable, Alex admired her young mistress's excellent horsemanship. She'd been surprised at Lady Cassandra's request for Appleton. Spirited stallions were not usually ridden by the "delicate" daughters of rich lords, and Lady Cassandra certainly looked the part. The bodice of her expensive riding habit fit snugly against Cassandra's slender ribcage down to her small waist, where the full skirt flowed to swirl around trim ankles. The bright whiteness of a lace cravat cascaded in waterfall folds against full breasts, lifting gently with each breath. Her ash-blonde hair was caught up under a tall riding hat. A flowing chiffon scarf looped loosely once around Cassandra's long neck before trailing behind her. Long, brown lashes framed brilliant blue eyes in an oval-shaped face that had been carefully protected from the sun. A sprinkling of light freckles, the bane of any aristocratic female, powdered her delicately sloped nose and high cheeks. Her full, rosy lips did not need any artificial color.

Alex had experienced a tremor when she held the hand of the haughty daughter of the Eighth Earl of Graywick, Lord Clayton Ellington Stonehurst, but she recognized what had happened. At three and twenty years of age, she knew where her inclinations lay, having enjoyed not too few tumbles in the hay with the innocent daughters of her father's friends — daughters who thought the chaste kisses and tender fondlings were all in fun, but which Alex took very seriously. She did not understand her own feelings, but accepted them with the innocence of a country lass. She often wished her mother, Emma, were still alive to talk to.

Emma had been an impoverished gentlewoman whose one chance at marriage was to a neighboring farmer, Matthew Ferrars. Although they were poor, Emma hoped that her daughter could be more than a simple farmer's wife. Besides providing the girl with a homespun version of her own classical education, Emma also taught Alex the ways of genteel society. Matthew had often despaired at the "book learning," but he loved his wife deeply and let her keep Alex out of the fields, even though he desperately needed the help. Because Alex was their only child, he was forced to hire seasonal labor, which cut deeply into their meager earnings. The three of them were very happy, however, until Emma died of influenza soon after Alex turned sixteen. Matthew was inconsolable. Neglected by its grieving tenant, the farm fell to ruin. Alex and her father were forced to move north to his brother's farm in West Yorkshire County, where he continued to languish. After a cold winter, Alex knew she could not remain an additional burden to her uncle, so at the age of eighteen she bid farewell to her father and her old way of life. She returned south to Cambridgeshire County to earn her keep.

Finding work was more difficult than Alex had imagined. She'd hoped to be employed as a governess, but soon discovered that no one wanted to hire a young woman without references to teach his children, no matter how well she could speak and write. Alex convinced herself she wouldn't be happy as a governess anyway and tried her hand at physical labor. She hired herself out to anyone who would take her. Discovering she enjoyed the work, Alex for once regretted her mother's insistence that she not farm the fields.

Alex began to pride herself on her unusual strength and the muscular body that soon developed. She realized that the advantage men had for doing hard work in the hot fields came not as much from their biology as from their attire. Before long, Alex cut her waist-length hair to its current short style and discarded cumbersome skirts for men's breeches. If her employers were scandalized by her attire, they soon forgot it. She was an excellent a worker with a growing list of references, and although she worked harder than most men, she could be paid less because of her sex. No one had offered permanent work, however, until ten months ago. She had spent a few days assisting a horse merchant at the local market in Fulbourn, and there she met James, the head groom for Stonehurst Manor. Seeing her natural ability with horses, he decided to hire her. She had not disappointed him.

Even after Cassandra and Appleton were long out of sight, Alex stood staring after them. In the four years between leaving her father and finding employment at Stonehurst Manor, she had had one brief affair with a scullery maid who thought it a lark to let a woman kiss her and send her body quivering to new heights with touches so intimate they made her swoon. She soon tired of the game, and told Alex never to bother her again or she'd inform the mistress of the house. It was not right, after all, for women to be doing such things, she'd said. Alex had not touched a woman since then; until, of course, she'd held Lady Cassandra's hand in hers. She sighed heavily as she took up her rake to continue mucking out the stable. She remembered too vividly the pleasure of caressing a woman's soft body. It would not do to develop a *tendre* for the young mistress of Stonehurst Manor. She tried to work even harder than usual to keep herself from distraction. And yet, the memory of Cassandra's rosy lips and slender neck haunted her.

As she rode away, Lady Cassandra thought of Alex. She resisted the temptation to look back to see if Alex was watching her. Why should it matter if she was? The woman was nothing but a stablemaid and a disgrace to womanhood as well. She wondered how long Alex had been working at the manor and why she hadn't noticed the woman before now. Because Appleton was usually brought to the house by Josh the stableboy, Cassandra rarely ventured down to the stable but surely she would have heard talk about a strange female? Not even Lizzie, who acted as Lady Cassandra's lady's maid and was a terrible gossip, had said anything. Trying not to dwell on the matter, Cassandra instead put her energies into an invigorating, April spring-morning ride across the estate.
    Late the same morning, a tired, but happy, Cassandra returned to the stable in a generous mood, eager to talk more to Alex and to satisfy her curiosity about the stablemaid. She was nowhere to be seen, and it would not do for the young heiress

to inquire after her without reason. Strangely, Lady Cassandra was deeply disappointed, and she was terse with the young lad who came to take Appleton from her. Flouncing up to the house in time for luncheon, she dismissed the strange Alex from her mind. Her attention turned instead to the fabrics she would choose for her new summer wardrobe. She couldn't wait to trade heavy velvet for light muslin and silk.

Weeks passed. Cassandra found herself busy with the traditional spring and summer fêtes and soirees being held throughout the Fulbourn district. Somehow, though, dancing in the arms of eligible young bachelors did not give her the pleasure it once had. At times she found herself almost repulsed by their touch, which confused her. Now and then, when a young gentleman would take her hand to lead her to dance, she would remember the fleeting moment when Alex held her hand. Her resulting shiver would make Cassandra's dance partner press her hand more tightly. She would then dazzle him with a brilliant smile, thinking that if he thought he had won her heart he was sadly mistaken. Cassandra was becoming quite the flirt!
 Her own formal debut, scheduled for midsummer, was approaching. The July 15 ball, the biggest and grandest in the countryside, would signify Lady Cassandra's official eligibility for marriage. She had convinced her parents not to give her a London season, for she much preferred the country. Besides, the few times she'd been to London, she had hated

the noise and the stench and the mass of swirling humanity. It made her feel small and insignificant, and that was something she didn't like.

Among the many preparations for the ball, special Siamese silk was ordered for a gown designed by Cassandra's seamstress. To Cassandra's delight, the first fitting showed the gown to be as beautiful on her as it was in the fashion sketches drawn by the seamstress.

"It is the most elegant gown I have ever seen," Cassandra exclaimed to her mother as they stood together before a full-length mirror.

"You do look perfectly lovely," Lady Elinor Stonehurst said with a smile. "You are sure to be the belle of the ball."

The gown's decolletage was cut deliciously low to expose Cassandra's generous cleavage. The short puffed sleeves were trimmed with expensive Belgian lace. The high waistline was gathered under her breasts with a silver satin sash; the gown then flowed slim and featherlight to Cassandra's ankles. The shimmering material was the color of sun-ripened raspberries, and the lace trimming blushed with palest pink. An overskirt of sheer pink muslin was threaded throughout with fine, glittering silver threads. Her feet would be encased in white, soft kid slippers with just the barest hint of a heel. An ivory fan, a lace-covered reticule, and long, white satin gloves would complete the outfit.

"I do wish the neckline were more modest, Cassandra," her mother said, frowning.

"No, mother, it is perfect. After all, I am eighteen now, and a woman. You don't need to treat me like a child."

Her mother sighed. "Yes, you're right. Would you like to wear my ruby and diamond necklace?"

Cassandra tilted her head left and right, imagining her ash-blonde curls gathered in a Grecian knot at the top of her head. She held her fingers to her throat.

"It would go perfectly with this dress. Thank you. I should like that." She gave her mother a kiss on the cheek.

"I think that you will be engaged before Christmas."

Before her mother could speak further, Cassandra dismissed the subject with a wave of her hand. "Let's not talk of that now. I want to look over the invitation list."

She stepped back from the mirror and allowed her seamstress to remove the dress. Cassandra did not want to think about being married.

With friends and relatives due to arrive a week before the ball, Cassandra rode twice each day, knowing she'd be pressed into duty once the house was full of guests.

Elinor had planned many activities for the week, and on the last afternoon before the arrival of her guests, Cassandra walked down to the stables. It was an impulsive decision, and she felt awkward, having not visited the stables since the early spring day she met Alex. Thankfully, she had not spoken to James. Now, in a riding habit of blue broadcloth, heedless of the dust swirling around the hem of her skirt, Cassandra wandered through the stableyard, hoping for a glimpse of the stablemaid, but she did not appear. Instead, a young groom hurried over as Cassandra paused uncertainly in the doorway.

"Can I help yer, milady?" the boy asked. His eyes bulged with curiosity at her presence.

Cassandra smiled. "Yes. Please saddle up Appleton. He's the black stallion."

As he hurried to do her bidding, Cassandra continued to look around. The tail form she hoped to see did not materialize. Perhaps it is her day off, she thought. The boy brought Appleton to her. Cassandra smiled her thanks and waved him away. She used the mounting block to swing unassisted onto the horse. With a light flick of her riding crop, she set Appleton into a steady canter.

The afternoon sky had begun to cloud over, but Cassandra was unconcerned. She knew she'd be back before the rain. She felt exhilarated by the brisk wind that scattered last autumn's fallen leaves in a swirling pattern like an intricate country dance. Appleton picked up his mistress's enthusiasm and matched it with his own, seeming to run faster and jump higher than ever before. When Cassandra saw the high hedge looming before them, she did not hesitate to guide Appleton over it. Just as they were clearing the hedge, booming gunfire startled the stallion. She felt his front legs go down as he stumbled his landing. Suddenly, her foot wrenched painfully out of the stirrup and she was up over the horse's head. Her stomach felt as if it was tumbling as she herself was, and she landed with a heavy thud on the hard ground. The jarring impact made her teeth chatter, and her neck snapped backward to an excruciating crack against the unyielding ground.

Slowly she regained her senses. Her ankle throbbed, her back and shoulders ached, and she was aware of being cradled in someone's strong arms. Her pounding head rested against something, oh, so soft. She was reluctant to open her eyes, wanting instead to revel in the feeling of contentment. She snuggled instinctively into the arms that held her and felt them tighten. Sighing demurely, she opened her eyes with a ladylike flutter and found herself staring into the most beautiful golden brown eyes she'd ever seen. She gasped as she recognized the features of the woman who held her — Alex! She felt an involuntary blush creep over her face and neck, and lowered her lashes to hide her discomfort.

"Milady, are you hurt?" Alex asked, her voice noticeably agitated. "You took quite a spill, but I don't think any bones are broken."

Cassandra opened her eyes to look again into Alex's tawny gaze. She felt herself blush furiously as she imagined Alex's hands roaming over her body to check for broken bones. Drowning in the intensity of that golden-brown stare, she melted back into Alex's arms. Is she going to kiss me, Cassandra thought, and waited for it to happen. Horrified at such ideas, she struggled to extricate herself from Alex's arms. Alex let her go easily and watched Cassandra shakily stand.

Cassandra spotted Appleton standing near a copse of trees, munching contentedly on the sweet green grass as if nothing had happened. She breathed a sigh of relief. It would have been heartbreaking to have to shoot her favorite stallion because he'd broken a leg. She approached him, conscious of Alex's presence beside her.

"Thank you for coming to my aid," she said to the silent woman. "I don't know what happened really. Appleton usually is not easily spooked. I heard gunshots. No one should be hunting now. Do you think it could be poachers?" She stopped speaking suddenly, aware that she was rambling. How could this woman beside her cause such a fluttering in her stomach? She reached out a tentative hand and touched Alex's arm. The soft hardness of Alex's muscles did not escape her notice. "I mean it when I say thank you, Alex."

Alex smiled then, and the sight took Cassandra's breath away. Her emotions were in a turmoil. She looked away and stumbled. Alex's hand shot out to steady her, but Cassandra jerked away, afraid to have the woman touch her. She avoided her gaze and made a big show of patting Appleton's neck and scolding him. Silently, she allowed Alex to help her mount, and without a backward glance, she cantered off toward the manor.

Again, Alex stood watching long after Lady Cassandra was out of sight. She was puzzled by the young mistress's actions, but she recognized in herself the long-dormant yearnings for a woman. A long time had passed since her affair with the scullery maid, since she'd dared to get involved with a woman. She knew it was ludicrous to harbor such desires for Lady Cassandra, who surely would be outraged if she knew. With a shrug of her strong shoulders, Alex strode purposefully over the rolling hills of the estate in the direction of the village, where she was due for a lesson with Harry, the blacksmith.

Alex was grateful that Harry had agreed to teach her his trade. It had taken much cajoling, but she'd won him over by promising to work for him for free during the course of her lessons. He seemed satisfied. Alex, he said, proved to be quicker than any lad he had taught before. She knew that the clothing she wore had shocked him at first, but before long, she had his respect. She was strong, and her gentle way with horses calmed even the most skittish of them.

Alex brushed the sweat-dampened hair from her forehead, leaving a black smudge. She was breathing heavily from the exertion of lifting the heavy hammer and from the intense heat of the forge. She noted Harry watching the rise and fall of her chest, unconsciously licking his lips. Ignoring him, Alex took off her heavy leather apron, hung it up, and then wiped her dirty hands on her breeches.

"Thanks, Harry. Same time next week?"

"Yeah," he replied with a wave of his hand.

Alex walked away, her long stride quick. The distance ahead meant she'd have to hurry to be back at Stonehurst Manor in time for dinner. The uppermost thought in her mind was to wash. She didn't want to take a chance that Lady Cassandra would see her, all sweaty and black with soot.

CHAPTER 2

As guests began to arrive for what would be the most important social event thus far in Lady Cassandra's life, she forgot everything except preparing for the ball. Appleton did indeed go unridden by his mistress. She was too busy trying on new gowns, hostessing afternoon teas, and entertaining not-often-seen friends and family. Her parents hoped that among the eligible bachelors invited she would choose one as a husband. Because Cassandra believed that they would not force her to marry someone she didn't love, she did not feel the same pressure as other young women in her society. By eighteen, most were already betrothed to rich, crotchety old men or to penniless young rakes with a desirable family name and title. Cassandra had no intention of following in those women's footsteps.

Nevertheless, she did find herself warming to the Marquess of Cavanaugh's heir, Alfred. His black hair, gloriously thick and curly, and brooding dark eyes hinted gypsy blood. His cheekbones were high and sculptured, his mouth full and sensuous. Tall and manly, he always dressed strikingly in stylish form-fitting clothes, but without the effeminate foppishness popular with so many of the *ton*. The one fault Cassandra noticed after spending time in his company was an apparent lack of intellect. The only subjects he could discuss at length were horses and cards. In fact, he was rather tiresome. Having herself been very well educated, more so than most aristocratic females, she expected her future husband to be equally suited to her intellectual standards. She didn't know if Lord Alfred was just trying to appear bored and indifferent, but she was determined to find out. She would never marry a dunderhead, even if a look from him sent her pulse racing.

The day before the ball, she invited Lord Alfred to go riding. He had expressed an interest in seeing her father's horses, so she decided to take him to the stables rather than have someone bring the horses to the house. She knew he'd want and expect a stallion like Appleton, but he'd have to settle for her papa's more gentle gelding. Appleton was, after all, hers and hers alone.

Cassandra wore her most flattering royal-blue riding habit and had Lizzie put her hair into face-framing ringlets. The riding hat's extra-long scarf of light powder blue looped sensuously around her neck. In the lacy white cravat of her shirt glimmered a sapphire brooch that matched her earrings and the brilliant sparkle of her blue eyes. The effort she took with her appearance was rewarded by Lord Alfred's indrawn breath as she descended the main staircase. She welcomed him with her smile. Placing a black-gloved hand delicately on his arm, she allowed him to escort her to the stables.

They chatted amicably about the fine weather and the number of guests, and Cassandra was admiring Lord Alfred's handsome profile when he suddenly stopped talking and stared in front of him. An unmistakably lewd smile curved his lips. Cassandra frowned and looked to see what had caused such an expression. She felt herself blush as she beheld Alex, whose male attire seemed even more disgraceful than the first time.

Alex did not see them right away; she had her back turned to them as she scooped oats into a bucket. Lord Alfred lasciviously admired the feminine curves shown off so well in the tight men's breeches. The girl wore a man's rose-colored cambric shirt that had seen better days, but the faded color was very flattering. The good-quality material hugged and draped her body in all the right places. Really!

Cassandra decided she'd have to say something to James after all. It was indecent that Alex wore such clothing, and it would not do to have male visitors thinking that this stablemaid was an easier mark than most female servants.

Cassandra slapped her riding whip against her skirt. No longer on Lord Alfred's arm, her free hand clenched and unclenched in her anger. She glared at Lord Alfred, but he was impervious to everything except Alex.

"Alex, saddle two horses immediately," she ordered harshly, satisfied to see the woman flinch in surprise.

"Milady, milord," Alex replied quickly as she turned to face them. "No one informed me that you would be riding today," she added apologetically. "I'll saddle Appleton immediately for the gentleman. Which horse will you ride, Lady Cassandra?"

She glared at the servant. "No one rides Appleton except me," she said, gritting her teeth. "You may saddle up Blue Mist for Lord Alfred."

Lord Alfred's eyes boldly traveled the length of Alex's muscular yet soft body. "You're a fine young woman," he drawled. "Why are you working in the stable instead of the parlor?"

Cassandra saw the look Lord Alfred gave Alex and could deduce what it meant. She was incensed. He was turning out to be the rudest man of the most common sort, and her morning was ruined. Her careful toilette was for naught; he had eyes only for the brazen Alex.

" 'Tis safer in the stable than in the parlor," the

stablemaid snapped. "At least in breeches instead of skirts I can escape more easily from the likes of you."

Lord Alfred gave a cruel sneer as he raised his riding whip to strike her. "How dare you speak to me in that manner!"

Cassandra grabbed his arm and stamped her foot. She found herself angry for Alex, although she knew a servant had no right to speak thus to someone of Lord Alfred's rank. "Guests at Stonehurst Manor do not raise their hands against anyone employed here," she said firmly. "I think our morning ride is out of the question. Please return to the house. I will speak with this girl. Do not let me catch you near her or I will have my papa order you to leave."

With a disdainful toss of her head, Cassandra turned her back on him and walked into the shadowed recesses of the stable. What an odious man he was! Not only was he a complete bore, but rude as well. She was trembling as she approached Appleton's stall to feed him an apple she had brought from the house. She felt rather than heard Alex behind her and turned to stare at the handsome young woman. The pity she had begun to feel at the treatment a woman of Alex's class had to endure from men disappeared. Cassandra gazed at a strong, confident woman who appeared unperturbed. Alex smiled at her and she smiled back.

"Milady, you do not have to protect me, but thank you. I am sorry your ride is ruined. Could you not take Appleton out alone?"

Momentarily, Cassandra's anger returned. "How

dare you even suggest that Lord Alfred ride Appleton?" she demanded. "If I had been my papa you would not have so quickly offered his horse."

Alex raised her eyebrows, but did not answer. The two women stood and stared at each other for a long while. Finally, Cassandra turned back to her stallion and stroked his soft nose. He snorted gently, as if he had caught the faint scent of the long-eaten apple on her gloved hand.

Cassandra's quiet voice broke the silence. "I'm sorry you had to endure that. I had no idea Lord Alfred was so rude."

"All men are like that, milady. They are schooled to respect women such as yourself, but those of us who work for a living must endure all sorts of unwelcome advances. I have learned to fend them off. You need not worry about me."

"Wouldn't it be easier for you if you dressed properly? Why do you insist on wearing men's clothes? And this stable is no place for a young woman. I can get you a position in the house."

Alex laughed. "Do you think clothes make a difference to men? Skirts or breeches, it's all the same. I would not be happy in the house. I am neither maid nor companion. I'm sorry if my attire offends you, milady, but it is most practical for me."

"You speak very well, Alex. What is your family background?"

The stablemaid shrugged. "My mother was a gentlewoman who taught me the ways of the gentry. She thought it would make my life easier. I know how to read and write, but it has been a long time since I've held a book in my hands."

"I'll bring you books from papa's library,"

Cassandra said impulsively as she walked out into the sunshine. "Take Appleton out for a ride, will you," she called. "He's been awfully neglected of late."

Alex followed her, too surprised at the order to reply. She had never been allowed to ride the horses to exercise them. She watched Lady Cassandra saunter from the stableyard, and then went to Appleton's stall to take him out. The bucket of oats stood forgotten outside the door. An order from the young mistress of the house was more important than one from James, even if he was the head groom.

Appleton was as eager to be ridden as Alex was to ride. She quickly saddled him with a man's saddle; no ridiculous lady's sidesaddle would suit her. Vaulting onto the horse's back to sit astride, Alex turned him out of the stableyard and toward the wide rolling hills of the estate.

Alex had immediately recognized the look on Lord Alfred's face. She'd seen it often enough since changing her profession and then her attire. These men, whether lord or peasant, viewed her as a novelty, but a woman nevertheless to be taken advantage of and used to satisfy their lust. Thus far, she'd been able to outwit them all.

Lady Cassandra was different. Alex only wanted to memorize her flushed cheeks and blazing eyes. She had watched Lady Cassandra nervously smacking the riding whip against her blue skirt and wanted to snatch up that hand and kiss it fervently.

She let Appleton have his head. His powerful muscles flexed and contracted beneath her own muscled thighs. Alex felt exhilarated, both from her encounter with Cassandra and from the feel of the wind on her face. Her gentle hands controlled the reins, guiding the animal farther from the house. She would be gone for hours, not returning until it was time for the midday meal.

CHAPTER 3

Lady Cassandra dressed carefully for her debut ball, but with little enthusiasm. She studied herself in the mirror and told herself she looked positively stunning. Her new silk gown was the color of sun-kissed raspberries; her shapely legs were faintly outlined beneath the thin fabric. Her shining blonde hair was coiled and curled and strung through with diamonds, and around her slim neck her mother's ruby and diamond necklace glittered. She took up her ivory fan and lace-covered reticule and descended the stairs to join her parents in the receiving line.

She greeted new and old guests and smiled until she thought her face would split in two. Bowing low and kissing her gloved hand, the men breathed in her subtle rose perfume and stared at her cleavage. She wanted to snatch her hand away. When Lord Alfred was presented she was icily correct and barely acknowledged his murmured greeting. Her parents arched their eyebrows in surprise, but Cassandra was too well bred to be openly rude. She kept her greeting to the marquess's heir just short of contemptuous. Her parents were wrong if they thought she had developed an affection for Lord Alfred. If they felt a twinge of disappointment, if they had been rather impressed by Lord Alfred's title and bearing and not at all adverse to the idea of a Stonehurst–Cavanaugh match, it would not be her problem. Many more eligible young men had come to the ball. Lord Alfred would not be making her a marchioness, she thought, and so be it. He himself seemed oblivious to her snub.

Finally, the last guest departed the receiving line. It was time for the family to enter the magnificent ballroom to officially begin the dancing. The crystal chandeliers and silver candelabra sparkled and glittered from the light of hundreds of candles. The entire ballroom was beautifully decorated with flowers from the Stonehurst Manor gardens. The room flashed with brilliant colors from the multihued clothing and precious jewels worn by the guests as they whirled and stepped in popular dances. Cassandra danced first with her father. Afterward, several young gentlemen clustered around her, and her dance card filled quickly. She did not rest for hours.

Lord Alfred too had signed Cassandra's dance card. She knew she had to dance with him at least once, out of politeness if nothing more. She didn't want to embarrass her parents with a scene. He presented her with a sweeping bow when he came to claim his waltz.

"Lady Cassandra. I believe this dance is mine."

She placed one gloved hand in his, the other on his shoulder. Grinning like a wolf, he whirled her onto the floor. She kept as much distance between them as was possible for such an intimate dance.

"You look very beautiful tonight," Lord Alfred complimented. "You outshine every other woman here."

Cassandra quietly murmured her thanks while she kept her eyes at a spot just above his left shoulder. She was almost rigid with her distaste.

"My dear, you mustn't be angry with me. Don't be jealous of that slattern in the stables. You are the one I am going to marry."

His statement renewed Cassandra's fury. She glared at the man. How presumptuous he was! "Don't you dare speak to me that way," she hissed. "It is hot in here. I would like to sit down."

Without waiting for an answer, she pulled out of Lord Alfred's grasp and headed toward the refreshment table. She could feel him watching her walk through the throng of guests. He treated her like he enjoyed her anger, she thought. She knew her rejection of him would make marrying her more of a challenge. She paused to look back at him. Another pretty young woman had caught his eye. He sauntered over to her, and Cassandra knew she was momentarily forgotten.

When next Cassandra noticed Lord Alfred, he was dancing with her mother. Then she saw him talking with her father, their heads bent together like conspirators. The sight gave her a prickly feeling. She decided to speak with her mother, but before she could move, another man claimed his dance.

At last Cassandra pleaded to be allowed to rest. The ballroom was stiflingly hot. Appearing suddenly at her elbow, Lord Alfred solicitously offered to obtain for her a lemonade. Refusing his overture of friendship, she decided to walk alone in the garden. She fanned herself vigorously as she exited unnoticed into the cooler night air. She quickly looked around to be sure no one had seen her, then hurried off toward a circle of tall yews. In the center of the trees, where once had stood a delicate wooden gazebo, the moonlight now glinted on a small replica of a Grecian temple. She smiled when she saw it, remembering her father's grudging acquiescence to the classical revival, which had become all the rage during the current reign of the Prince Regent in this year of 1813.

She sighed as she sat on a marble bench, careful not to crush her silk gown more than necessary. It was still just after midnight; the festivities would not end until dawn. Cassandra surprised herself by wishing the night were over. No longer was it enjoyable to be the center of attention, especially for men interested only in her money or her figure.

She leaned her head against a cool marble column, closed her eyes, and fanned herself languidly. The garden smelled wonderfully of a myriad of flowers; the night noises were gently soothing. Suddenly, the sound of gravel being crushed beneath walking feet intruded on her thoughts. She frowned as she opened her eyes to glare at whomever dared interrupt her peace. A tall dark figure loomed in the doorway, hesitant. Cassandra opened her mouth to order the intruder away, then realized it was a woman, one who dressed in men's clothing.

"Alex," she breathed, "what are you doing here? Shouldn't you be sleeping? 'Tis very late."

The figure moved slowly into the miniature temple and sat on the bench across from her. The stablemaid's presence was overpowering. Confused by her feelings, Cassandra nervously twirled her fan. Why should a female servant affect her so? She allowed her eyes to sweep over Alex's lithe frame, noting how the rolled-up sleeves of her shirt revealed powerful forearms. The shirt was not buttoned to the top, and she glanced at the pulse in the hollow of Alex's throat and then at her generous cleavage. Blushing, Cassandra lowered her lashes and selfconsciously cleared her throat.

Alex came out of her reverie and stretched her long legs. She crossed her arms and a slow smile transformed her face. Her perfect white teeth gleamed in the moonlight. "Why, milady," she belatedly answered, "I didn't know you were so concerned. I come here often, but tonight I especially wanted to hear the music."

Cassandra looked toward the house as the strains of another waltz drifted through the night. She briefly wondered if anyone had missed her yet. Looking back at Alex, she found herself admiring the woman's independence and defiant spirit. It occurred to her all at once that her own existence was unexciting and confined. How could young women of her class think that the only thing in life was to marry a man picked by their parents and to have a house full of children? What would it be like to be on her own? To have the freedom of her male cousins? Or of Alex?

As Cassandra continued to stare at Alex, it seemed that the woman's eyes had become more bold. They searched her face and then slowly, oh so slowly, traveled down her neck to the swell of her bosom. After lingering there in a caress that might have lasted minutes, Alex's gaze swept back to Cassandra's face. Alex must have been oblivious to what had just occurred, Cassandra told herself, dismissing her own thoughts as foolishness. A woman surely would not gaze upon her as a man would.

The silence between them lengthened. Very slowly, Alex leaned forward. Her hands raised purposefully, as if to take hold of Cassandra's arms. At that moment, the tinkling laughter of a lady and the heartier laugh of a gentleman boomed in the still air. Cassandra leapt guiltily to her feet and fanned herself vigorously. She was breathing heavily. Alex lowered her hands and leaned back languorously against the wall of the temple. She continued to remain silent.

There was a murmur of voices as the intruders approached the hidden temple — two lovers intent on the privacy of the romantic place. She knew that as soon as the they turned the corner, they would see her ... and Alex.

"You must leave at once," she hissed, her eyes darting to the path that lead to the temple.

"As you wish, my *lady*," Alex replied, putting a sarcastic emphasis on the last word. "I would not want to humiliate you before your guests." The look she gave Cassandra was as much an insult as if Alex hadn't looked at her at all.

Fuming, Alex chose not to exit the temple using the doorway. Instead, she used her long legs to step over the temple's short wall and disappear into the bushes. The brutalized branches crackled back into place. Alex's angry stride took her toward the stables — her "proper" place. She realized then that her dear mother had unwittingly done her a great disservice by educating her in the finer things of life — music and books and conversation. Alex would never walk in the circles where such things were appreciated. She was a misfit, caught between two worlds, neither of which was hers. As she disappeared into the night, Alex heard surprised voices greet the "lady." She did not hear Cassandra's reply.

She sighed as she thought back to her first glimpse of Lady Cassandra in the temple. Hazy moonlight had caught the silver threads in Cassandra's gown and made them glimmer; her diamonds were brilliant flashes of light. She had been speechless as she gazed upon the young mistress, forgetting the subservience she should show. At that moment, Lady Cassandra had been no longer her mistress, but a woman to be admired and loved.

Cassandra woke late the day following her parents' ball. Her head ached and her eyes hurt from the sun glaring mercilessly through the open windows of her room. Someone had unthinkingly parted the heavy brocade curtains. She woke with a bad taste in her mouth. Cassandra couldn't remember when she'd had a more miserable night. Her debut ball, and she'd hated every minute of it. She looked over at the armoire. The beautiful, expensive gown lay crumpled in a heap on the floor and she didn't care. The way she felt now, she didn't care if she never attended another ball. All she could think about was going somewhere far away. Maybe her parents would let her visit Aunt Sophia, her papa's sister who lived near Scotland on her own estate in Northumberland. It would be nice and gloomy there to match her mood. She heard a tentative knock. Lizzie entered the room, carrying a tray.

"Milady?" the maid began timidly.

Cassandra sat up angrily. "Who told you to open those curtains?" she began, but looking at the dull expression on Lizzie's coarse face reminded her that human contact, especially of this sort, was the last thing she wanted right now. "Oh, just leave the tray on the table and go away. Tell Mother I have a dreadful headache and will remain abed today. I will ring if I have further need of you."

Lizzie placed the tray on the bedside table and gave a quick curtsy before hastily leaving the room. Lady Cassandra had never before spoken to her so sharply.

Cassandra ignored the tempting smell of hot cocoa and fresh-baked bread spread with butter and marmalade. With a sigh, she fell backward into the soft feather pillows and closed her eyes. In spite of what the maid might believe — and she knew there would be talk below stairs — it was not Lord Alfred who occupied her thoughts, but Alex. Her memory of the night before was so vivid she thought she could smell even now Alex's soapy clean, slightly horsey scent that she was beginning, with each encounter, to recognize. Was it her imagination or had Alex wanted to kiss her?

The reminiscence took her back to the miniature temple. Again she felt the gentle night air surround her and heard the music quietly flowing out over the garden. She saw the silhouette that became Alex and felt the tall woman sit across from her. This time, however, when Alex leaned forward, no voices disturbed them and her lips touched Cassandra's, featherlight at first and then more bold. The sensation was so real that Cassandra gasped and opened her eyes, fully expecting Alex to be standing beside the bed. She closed her eyes and touched her fingers to her lips and then brought them down over her throat and to her breasts, where they lingered as she caressed herself softly. She slept, and her dreams were scandalous.

* * * * *

Alex did not have the luxury of lying abed until the late morning hours. She had been up at dawn, having had only a few hours of troubled sleep. She worked that morning with an angry fervor. Lady Cassandra was in her thoughts. She could visualize with intense clarity the way the young mistress of Stonehurst had appeared in the romantic darkness of the Grecian temple. She was the most beautiful woman Alex had ever seen, but that didn't diminish the anger Alex still felt at Cassandra's curt dismissal. Unbidden, Alex had allowed herself to believe Lady Cassandra looked upon her as more than a servant. How wrong she was!

As Alex began to scrub down the family's barouche, her anger turned inward on herself. That she could have been foolish enough to think for a moment that Cassandra cared one whit for her was the most ignorant thing she had ever done. She vowed that she would never humiliate herself in such a way again. To ensure this, she determined to do whatever was necessary to avoid seeing Lady Cassandra. It would mean an end to her reading, for Cassandra surely would no longer borrow books from the library for her.

"So be it!" she said aloud.

Alex knew she had to banish all thoughts of ash-blonde hair and sapphire eyes from her mind.

CHAPTER 4

It was many weeks before Cassandra saw Alex again. She had avoided going to the stables because she was confused and afraid of her own thoughts. She wished she could talk to someone, but instinctively knew that even her own mother wouldn't understand. Alex occupied her thoughts constantly. If her parents puzzled over her quiet mood, they wisely refrained from questioning her. If her coming-out ball did not bring about the hoped-for results, they said nothing. Societal conventions dictated that a young woman of her age and stature should soon be wedded, but her parents were loving and indulgent and, thankfully, would not force her into a loveless marriage.

One late September afternoon, she decided to ride unaccompanied through the estate grounds. The day started out beautifully. Though the coming autumn brought a crisp chill to the air, Cassandra stayed warm in a Shetland wool riding habit of silver-gray. Her black riding hat was adorned with a swooping gray and white ostrich feather. Suddenly, unexpected storm clouds began to gather in the darkening sky. Having ridden farther than she had intended, Cassandra realized she would not make it back to the manor before the rain fell. Appleton was already showing signs of skittishness, which meant the storm would be bad. Somewhere near the border of her papa's land was an abandoned hunting lodge, and she led the horse into the dark woods to look for the crumbling structure.

The clouds unleashed a deluge of rain before she found the lodge, and she was soaked to the skin when she finally saw the outline of a building in front of her. The crashing thunder of nearby lightning caused the stallion to prance nervously along the muddied path, making him difficult to control. The exhausted rider was thankful as she led Appleton into the welcome shelter of the lodge. The roof was broken in several places, and the wind blew through the broken windows. Her teeth chattering, Cassandra moved toward what appeared to be the driest spot and wondered if she would catch her death before the storm ended.

Settling her horse into the dry and dusty corner, Cassandra stood near him, hoping that the steaming heat from his body would in turn warm her. Her sodden riding habit clung heavily to her body, and she didn't feel she would ever be warm again. Her once-elegant hat was ruined, its jaunty ostrich feather looking now more like the wet tail of a forlorn, scraggly kitten. Sighing, she sank to the ground and tucked her riding skirt around her cold legs.

She had just fallen into an uneasy slumber when Appleton jolted her awake. He neighed loudly and, struggling, rose on all four legs. In the gloom she discerned a figure walking toward her, leading a horse. For a moment she experienced a sharp terror, but then she recognized Alex. How did that woman always manage to find her? Numb with cold, Cassandra shivered uncontrollably.

"My God, Alex!" she exclaimed, very unladylike. "How did you find me? Here, of all places?"

"I know you often ride far across the estate. When the alarm was given that you'd not come back I thought I could find you first. You are shivering, milady."

Cassandra laughed lightly. "Of course I am shivering. I am soaked to the skin." She began to rise unsteadily to her feet, but Alex stopped her.

"Please, milady, we cannot leave yet. I just barely made it through the rain myself."

"That's all right, then." Cassandra's teeth chattered. "I'm so cold I don't think I could stay on my horse."

Alex reached out and handed her a horse blanket, which Cassandra wrapped around herself. In its meager, though welcome, warmth, she made herself as comfortable as possible. Alex gently urged Appleton away and he walked over to the horse she had ridden. The horses touched noses and moved close together. Beating steadily on the roof, the pouring rain lulled Cassandra toward sleep again. Alex knelt down and gathered her into strong arms. The two women were silent.

"I am beginning to feel warm again," Cassandra said after a while. Her mouth was near Alex's neck.

Alex tightened her grip and nuzzled Cassandra's damp hair. "I was afraid I wouldn't find you in time. I couldn't have borne it."

"You take a lot of liberties, Alex. You frighten me at times. The feelings you awaken in me are strange. We shouldn't be here together like this."

"But it feels so right to hold you in my arms. I will take you home soon — when the rain stops. You tremble, milady?"

"Oh, don't call me 'milady' or 'Lady Cassandra' when we're alone, Alex." Cassandra spoke harshly to hide her confusion. "You may call me Cassie, but be careful where you use it. It wouldn't do for people to think you've become too familiar with the earl's daughter."

She burrowed deeper into Alex's arms. Alex was correct — it did feel right to be in her arms. Cassandra breathed in the musky odor of sweat and horse and rain and somehow it did not offend her. She knew that she, too, must smell of horse and wet earth. If her very proper mother could see her now she would surely swoon. Cassandra made a soft sound and found herself looking into Alex's golden-brown eyes. Her lips parted involuntarily, and, with a groan, Alex placed her mouth on Cassie's. The kiss was gentle, tentative. Cassandra pulled away, then moved forward again, her arms going round Alex's neck as the kiss deepened and took her senses away. The blanket slipped unnoticed from her shoulders, and Alex gripped her arms until they ached.

Cassandra pushed away again. "Stop, Alex! What are you doing? How can you kiss me that way? It is what a man does with a woman."

Alex continued to hold her. "Please ... milady ... Cassie. Do not pull away," she begged. "I know you feel the same."

Cassandra struggled to her feet. She knew the other woman spoke the truth. Silently she held out her hand, which Alex took as she stood. They stared at each other, breathing hard. With a mutual sigh they clasped each other and kissed again, this time with more passion. Without knowing how, they were suddenly down on the spread blanket. Alex had unbuttoned Cassie's long-sleeved jacket. Her work-roughened hands caressed Cassie's breasts, causing her nipples to harden and strain against the silken material of her shirt. Cassie moaned as Alex lifted her wet skirt and touched her legs through the lace and silk of her pantalettes. It seemed only a matter of minutes before she was completely divested of her clothing. She did not notice the chill in the air; her body felt as if on fire. When Alex lay her own hot naked body on hers, Cassie knew she'd not feel cold again.

* * * * *

The rain continued to fall, its muted drumming providing a sensual, musical background. The two horses made gentle noises, nuzzling and comforting each other. In the dusty corner, the two women learned different ways of comfort.

Alex already knew what gave women pleasure, but Cassie's innocent fingers seemed to take on a life of their own as they explored the hidden places of Alex's muscular body. She instinctively touched Alex the way she touched herself, late at night, in the lonely privacy of her big bed. Alex allowed herself to enjoy Lady Cassandra's fluttering fingers, before suddenly sitting up and pushing her down on the blanket to kiss the tender mouth. Alex's hands roamed over soft skin; she nuzzled Cassandra's sweet-smelling throat.

Cassie moved in response, clutching Alex's shoulders as new sensations coursed through her body. Alex ran her fingers along Cassie's satin-smooth thighs. Cassie moaned and instinctively thrust her hips forward. Alex sucked on a tender nipple as she let her fingers slide into the wetness between Cassandra's squirming legs. She slowly inserted two fingers deep into virginal recesses, causing the other woman to gasp. Cassandra stilled momentarily to revel in the mysterious feelings, then began to move her hips. Alex moved her fingers in and out and flicked her tongue over Cassie's flushed, burning body. With her mouth and her fingers, she drove Cassandra to heights of ecstasy never felt before in the lady's own self-exploratory caresses.

Cassandra moaned loudly as her body shook with the intensity of her orgasm. She clutched Alex's shoulders in a strong, talonlike grip. Alex kissed

Cassie, pushing her tongue deeply into the woman's mouth as her fingers continued their soft caress. Her other arm cradled Lady Cassandra's head. Both were breathing heavily and sweating profusely despite the cold. Cassandra was shaken to her very core by the physical sensations she had just felt.

She rested on the blanket, letting the tremors diminish. She couldn't in her wildest fantasies have imagined such an intense experience. Alex lay on Cassie's breasts and listened to the rapid beating of her heart. Cassandra absently ran her fingers through Alex's thick, soft hair. When she began to feel a chill, she moved Alex so she was covered with the other woman's body. They kissed, Cassandra's hands rubbing up and down Alex's strong back. She curled one leg up over Alex's buttock and slid her toes back and forth on Alex's leg. Silently and gently she eased Alex aside so that their positions were reversed. Slowly, she began to imitate what Alex had done, hesitatingly at first, then with more confidence.

Alex gasped in pleased surprise, and leaned back to enjoy the feel of Cassie's mouth on her breasts. When Cassie tenderly and tentatively moved her tongue over Alex's stomach and then lower, Alex wondered briefly if the lady was as innocent as she seemed. Lady Cassandra's mouth stopped short of Alex's curly triangle of hair, then moved back up to tease Alex's fully erect nipples. It seemed like hours before Cassandra's hands stopped their exploration of Alex's muscular body and one settled between Alex's throbbing legs.

Alex gave herself up to the sensations she had not felt except by her own hand. She cried out once as her body tensed beneath Cassie's fingers, then lay still for a moment. Suddenly, she took hold of Cassandra's shoulders and pulled her down for a deep kiss. They lay wrapped in each other's arms, absorbing warmth. Alex pulled Cassandra's riding skirt over them. For several minutes, only the sound of the lessening rain, their deep breathing, and the shuffling horses filled the abandoned hunting lodge.

Cassandra sighed. "I feel as if I'm made of melting snow. You are a surprise, my Alex."

Alex grinned. "May I say the same of you, Cassie." She pulled her closer. "Is it possible I am in love with you? Does that shock you?"

"No. Nothing could shock me now." Cassandra laughed, running the tips of her perfect oval nails across Alex's collarbone. "Who taught you what you know?"

"I needed no teacher," Alex answered. She rose on one elbow and smiled. "But you, milady, who taught you?"

Cassandra could not answer, but she felt the blood rush to her checks. Alex did not see her blush, for the room was very dark.

They stood and dressed without speaking, stopping only for quick kisses. Their eyes glowed catlike in the gloom. The rain had stopped and the horses were impatient, as if thinking of their warm stable and plentiful oats. Alex helped Cassandra mount and then hoisted herself up on her own horse, sitting astride.

In companionable silence they allowed the horses to take their own lead, knowing the animals' instincts would take them home better than any direction from their riders. The moon began to peek out from behind heavy gray clouds and sporadically light their path. The rain fell in a soft mist. Lady Cassandra's voice shattered the stillness, though she spoke softly.

"No one taught me either," she said.

"You learned the way I did then," Alex answered with a grin. "It seems to come from within. I only know that no man could make me feel that way, and I have no desire for men."

"Tell me," Lady Cassandra asked, "is your name really Alex?"

Her companion laughed, surprised at the change in subject. "My mother named me Alexandra, after her grandmother. I began to call myself Alex when I discarded my feminine clothing. Somehow Alexandra did not sound right while I wore breeches."

"Cassandra and Alexandra. We sound like sisters."

Alex did not reply, for at that moment they heard a shout. A lantern held aloft suddenly illuminated them. As their eyes adjusted to the sudden brightness, they saw it was James, the head groom, and some other male servants who had been sent out as a search party. The young heiress, ever the lady even in her bedraggled state, bowed her head to acknowledge the babble of excited voices.

"I'm safe and well, as you can see." She turned to smile at Alex. "Alex found me in the old hunting lodge. I had stopped there to get out of the storm. Thank you for your efforts. I'm sure Papa will appreciate it."

"Indeed, milady," James replied. "Yer father were very concerned, 'e was. Let me light yer way back." He glanced curiously at Alex, as if wondering why she would have searched on her own.

At the house, Cassandra allowed Alex to help her dismount. Her hand burned where they touched. With James standing by and Lord and Lady Stonehurst rushing out the door, the two women could not talk. They exchanged a secret, knowing look before Lady Cassandra was swept into her mother's arms and hustled into the house for a warm, rose-scented bath and a hot beverage liberally laced with brandy.

Alex took Appleton to the stable and lovingly rubbed him down for the night before giving him and the horse she'd ridden an extra serving of oats. She then retired to her simple room above the stable. Stripping, she dipped a sponge into a battered tin bucket and washed herself quickly with the chilly water. Shivering in the damp air, Alex dressed in a clean nightshirt and crawled into her cold bed. Exhausted, she slept immediately.

In her luxurious room, Cassandra dropped gratefully onto her bed, which had been warmed with a hot brick. It had taken all her imagination to appease her parents' questions and then plead fatigue so she could be left in peace. She felt slightly giddy from the brandy her papa insisted she drink. Drawing the eiderdown covers close around her, she felt herself blushing in the darkness as she remembered the way she and Alex had touched.
    Her thoughts were racing and she knew it would

be hours before she slept. What she and Alex had done was scandalous, and she tried to tell herself it was wrong. She felt again the gentleness of Alex's hands and tasted her sweet mouth. She unwittingly remembered Lord Alfred's lascivious behavior. His touch would have been crude, and the thought made her shudder. She recalled the other men she had encountered in the last couple of years and couldn't think of a single one who could make her heart race the way Alex did. How was she ever going to convince her parents that she couldn't possibly marry?

    In the weeks that followed, Cassandra spent more and more time with Alex. It was difficult to explain to her parents her sudden interest in the happenings at the stables. For a week or so, an unexpected litter of kittens born in one of the empty stalls was as good an excuse as any. Then it seemed that Appleton was developing a cold, so his mistress just had to spend time with him. Soon, however, Cassandra didn't offer any explanation at all. She would follow as Alex performed her daily chores, all the while reveling in the beauty of the woman's muscular body.
    Alex took the time to teach Cassandra how to saddle up her own horse. At first she frowned in distaste. Why would she need to know such a thing? Alex was persistent however, and Cassandra had to admit a certain pride when she finally accomplished the feat on her own. Her parents would be appalled if they knew their daughter sullied her hands doing

the work of a stablehand. She enjoyed her time with Alex, but, eventually, the stables no longer held her interest. She knew Alex's routine by heart, and could almost have done it herself.

Although Alex had told her that she'd never be happy working in the house, Cassandra still tried to think of some way to entice her there so they could be together. She even considered dismissing Lizzie and making Alex her lady's maid, which made Alex laugh. All of Cassandra's suggestions fell on deaf ears. Alex just would not give up her freedom to dress as a man.

The two women would sneak kisses in the dark recesses of the stables, sometimes in Appleton's very stall. The urge to go tumbling down into the sweet-smelling hay was overwhelming, but they never had an opportunity to repeat their afternoon in the rain-soaked hunting lodge. Alex had to spend so much time doing chores, and besides, they never knew when someone might come into the stables. Finally, Cassandra could stand it no longer.

"Alex," she said one day as she stepped gingerly around a pile of manure, her nose wrinkling at the foul odor. "We must see each other privately." She wanted to feel her softness against her again. "Why won't you consent to work in the house? Then we could be together always and no one would question it. My parents are beginning to wonder why I'm here all the time."

Alex took some tack off the wall and began oiling the leather. She nodded her head toward a wooden chest. Before sitting, Cassandra spread a horse blanket out on the chest to protect her delicate muslin dress of lavender and pink. Alex continued to work in silence, as if contemplating Cassie's words.

Cassandra took off her poke bonnet and placed it carefully on the chest beside her. "Are you listening to me?" she queried, frustrated.

Alex glanced up and smiled before returning her attention to the saddle. "I always listen to you, Cassie. You know why I won't work in the house. I am not a domestic. I love being outside and I love my work."

"No one would question me asking a maid into my room, but they certainly would a stablehand. What can we do? Do you expect me to come skulking out to your room in the middle of the night?"

"Oh no, milady, never that!" Alex exclaimed sarcastically. She rubbed the saddle furiously. "I would never ask you to soil yourself so."

Cassandra gave an impatient toss of her head and hopped up. The motion sent her bonnet rolling off the chest and into a dark corner. She was impervious to the dust rising around the hem of her gown as she childishly stamped her foot.

"You are impossible to talk to. Don't you understand my position? I want us to be together, but you have to help me. I'm not saying your quarters aren't good enough, but it's much too risky. You won't come to my bedroom at night. Can't you understand? Sneaking kisses just isn't enough anymore."

In the silence that followed, Cassandra glanced around looking for her bonnet. So many of her clothes were being ruined by the dirt of the stables.

She was sure Lizzie talked about it, and that made her more determined to get Alex into the house.

Alex sighed. "No matter what we could do, Cassie, it would always be too risky. We come from two different stations in life and we can never bring them together. It would be better if we stopped seeing each other altogether."

Alex was careful not to look at Lady Cassandra. She knew her resolve would be broken if she saw the hurt in Cassie's blue eyes, but she had lain awake many a night thinking that their love could never survive. Too many obstacles barred their way. Even if she did consent to work in the manor house, it would not be any easier to get together, despite what Lady Cassandra thought. The young heiress didn't realize just how vicious and nosy house servants could be.

"How can you say that? I thought you loved me. If we love each other we can do anything."

Alex turned to Lady Cassandra and asked viciously, "It's easy for you to ask me to change my life, isn't it? But what about you? Would you be prepared to give up the life you lead? The fine gowns, the comfortable bed, the servants answering your every beck and call? Would you give that up for me? Would you? Would you be happy running away, sleeping in fields or any rundown shelter we could find? Would you work scrubbing out someone else's kitchen pots?" She turned her back to Lady Cassandra's stricken face. "Men would be free to do what they will with you then. No one would protect you."

"Alex ... Alex, what are you saying?" Lady Cassandra cried out, the anguish in her voice heartbreaking.

"You're an intelligent woman, Cassie. You've had a better education than most. You must know we cannot go on this way. I wouldn't fit into your drawing rooms any more than you'd fit into my haylofts. Can you see me mincing about in a fragile gown of imported silk, fluttering a fan and my eyelashes?"

"You're too cruel. If you loved me, you would do it."

Alex finished oiling the saddle and hung it on the wall with slow deliberation. She turned and confronted Cassandra's brilliant blue stare. "And if you loved me, you would do it my way."

Alex turned and walked out of the stable, blinking in the bright sunshine. She knew Lady Cassandra stood immobile inside, but she refused to look back. It had been absurd even to think they could be together. Their worlds were too different — one of them the heiress to a large fortune, the other a common stablehand, educated perhaps, but still a peasant by anyone's standards. She needed to vent her frustration, so she found James and asked if she could go into town to work with Harry.

Cassandra ran sobbing up to the manor house. She left Lizzie speechless as she brushed past her on the stairs. Once in her room, she unceremoniously flung herself onto her bed. She knew Alex's words were true, but she didn't want to believe them. The intensity of her emotions exhausted her and she fell into a restless sleep, only to be woken by Lizzie shaking her none too gently.

"Ooh mistress, wot 'ave you done? Look at yer gown, all covered with dirt and 'ay. 'ave you been to the stables again? An' sleepin' in it too! Yer papa be askin' fer you. Let me change you. Quick!"

The maid stripped off the lavender- and pink-striped muslin gown, clucking over the brown stains on the hem. She couldn't keep the greedy curiosity out of her eyes. Cassandra suspected that Lizzie talked about her forays to the stables to keep company with the strange female who insisted on dressing like a man. The gossip below stairs was probably speculative and none too kind, but Cassandra could not hide her red, swollen eyes and the tears that would no doubt fuel the nasty gossip. She had never insisted on getting a proper lady's maid — one who would have known her place, been loyal, and not talked about her betters — and she hoped she would not regret this bitter mistake.

Cassandra listlessly let Lizzie dress her in a cream-colored satin dress. One of her favorites, its transparent overskirt was embroidered with tiny brown flowers, the high waist tied with a chocolate-brown sash. Lizzie swiftly combed her mistress's hair into a presentable style, then stayed behind to tidy up as Cassandra descended the wide staircase and proceeded to her father's library. She tried to smile as he turned to face her, a severe frown on his face. He motioned for her to close the door.

"Cassandra," he began sternly. "Your mother and I have always indulged you, a little too much I think, but now we must insist that you seriously consider marriage. There has been talk about you and that creature who works in our stables . . ."

"Talk? About Alex and me?" Cassandra was incredulous. "What sort of talk?"

"My dear," Lord Stonehurst continued, "I cannot have your good name bandied about. You are old enough now for a husband and a home of your own."

"I don't ... understand," Cassandra stammered. "Alex and I have a friendship. Why should that force me into marriage?"

"Alexandra, or Alex, as you insist on calling her, will no longer be working for us. I told James to give her a month's wages and send her on her way." Cassandra was shocked into silence as her father continued to speak. "We do not need such a scandalous female here. If I had known you were getting so close, I would have dismissed her weeks ago. That girl is not the kind of friend you should have. You should associate with those of your own class."

"Papa!" Lady Cassandra wailed. "You cannot do this! Alex has done nothing wrong. It is so unfair."

"It is not right for you to have such a friendship with a servant. I ignored it when you took books from the library for her and when you insisted on following her around like a puppy, but now it's gone too far. There are things about her that you would not understand. She is not a normal woman."

"What things?" Cassandra demanded. "Is it because she refuses to submit to men? Because she believes in comfort above the dictates of fashion? Because she is strong and independent?"

Lord Stonehurst spoke angrily. "It is obvious that she has been filling your head with nonsense. I will not have you in her company. I forbid you to see her."

Trembling, Cassandra stood before him in contained rage. She had never before felt anything akin to hatred for her papa. Suddenly, all the obstacles she and Alex faced did not matter. She knew that she would give up everything to be with her and that she had to plan carefully. Cassandra forced herself to stay calm. She looked coolly upon her father and said, "As you wish. I was tiring of the novelty anyway. Such an odd girl ... I will see you at dinner?"

If her papa was surprised at her easy capitulation, he gave no sign of it. He dismissed her with a curt nod of his head. She wanted to slam the library door behind her, but she forced herself to close it gently. She glanced at his formidable butler standing a respectful distance from the doorway, but she thought she detected a guilty flicker in his dark eyes. She could just imagine what he would tell the others. With a disdainful sniff in his direction, she haughtily ascended the curving staircase and entered her room, closing the door with a resounding bang. Too angry to succumb to a fit of feminine vapors, she sat in her window seat and plotted her course of action.

Somehow, she had to get a message to Alex before James threw her off the grounds. Cassandra knew that, in his present mood, her papa would not give Alex the courtesy of spending one last night at Stonehurst Manor, despite the fact that the sun was already setting. The beautiful streaks of lavender and pink in the twilight blue sky did not stir her romantic heart. She could trust no one. She knew her own maid talked about her behind her back with a viciousness that went beyond normal curiosity of a servant for her betters. Cassandra had to get to the stables one more time. She decided it would be best to stroll casually down on the pretext of seeing her beloved Appleton.

It was practically dark when she arrived. She drew her midnight blue cloak tightly around her; beneath it she had hidden a bag filled with money and with food filched from the kitchen. A stableboy gawked at her in surprise, but she ignored him and walked sedately to Appleton's stall, quieting the horse with a carrot and a lump of sugar. As he munched contentedly, Cassandra strained her eyes in the gloom, searching for any sign of Alex. Behind her, a shadowy form crept into the darkness of the stable. Cassandra gasped as a hand closed over her arm.

"'Tis only I," Alex whispered. "I should not be here. I was told to leave before sunset, but somehow I knew you'd come."

"Oh, Alex," Cassandra whispered back. "I was hoping to find you. Here, I brought you some food." Alex put her arms around her lover's waist, but Cassie pulled back. "We have little time," she warned. "In four weeks I will meet you at my Aunt Sophia's home. She lives in Northumberland, near Alnwick. We can be safe there for a while. I've put a note for her inside the bag, and one for you with the directions to Dovecote."

Alex was skeptical. "How can you be sure she will let us live with her? She will feel obliged to tell your father where you are."

"She's a bit eccentric herself, and a spinster. I believe she will be glad of the company and will find this an adventure." Staring into Alex's sad eyes, she added, "And what other choice do we have?"

At that, they moved into the shadows and melted into each others' arms. Cassie could feel herself tremble, and she wished circumstances were different. Alex lifted Cassie's chin and gently brought their lips together. Cassandra clung to her with desperation and kissed her with a sense of foreboding.

"I'm so afraid, Alex. Promise me you will be careful. It will take you days to get to my aunt's house. It's practically to Scotland. I wish I had enough money to send you by coach."

Alex smoothed back Cassandra's hair. "Fear not, my love. I have lived many years on my own, and I know how to travel the roads. I count the days until we can be together. You know I will take care of myself. Now, I must go before we're caught. I love you, Cassie."

She caught Alex's hand and brought it to her cheek. "I love you too, Alex. Godspeed."

She dropped Alex's hand and whirled away before Alex could see the tears in her eyes. She walked rapidly toward the house, her dark cloak billowing behind her. She didn't know how she would get through the next few weeks, but she knew it would take careful planning before she could join Alex. She wished too that she were as confident about her aunt taking them in as she had pretended. She could only hope that her letter of introduction would suffice.

Dinner that night was an interminable affair. Cassandra could barely choke down a few mouthfuls from each of the five courses. It was hard to act as if all were well when the rage and despair she felt from the turn of events warred within her. She wondered if her father had said anything to her mother, but it didn't seem likely. When the time finally came to leave her father alone with his port and cigar, she fled to her room. Cassandra had no desire that night for embroidery, the pianoforte, or idle chitchat with her mother.

It was after midnight before she fell into an uneasy slumber, her dreams haunted by visions of Alex being set upon by highwaymen. The physical discomfort brought on by her mental anguish was not alleviated by her soft, down-filled comforter or scented sheets.

Alex did not have such a troubled night. She traveled on foot for many hours before hunger and tired feet forced her to retire to the shelter of a copse of trees. Under the moonlight, she read Cassandra's note and ate the thick bread and tangy cheese from the Stonehurst kitchen. Cassie had even managed to include a flask of strong wine. The instructions were simple—she was to travel to Dovecote, Aunt Sophia's modest estate, and give her the letter of reference written in Lady Cassandra's own hand. Lady Cassandra was sure her aunt would have some sort of employment for Alex until Cassandra herself could arrive and explain the whole situation.

Alex smiled as she turned gold guineas over in her hands. Cassie doesn't know the cost of things, she thought. Not only was this more than enough money to take the coach, but, along with the month's pay she had received, it was more money than Alex had ever possessed. She determined to guard the money well and save it for when they were together. They would certainly need it. Cassandra would no longer have a father who indulged her every whim.

The October night was cold but not uncomfortable. Alex wrapped her cloak around her and nestled into a crackling pile of leaves. She slept immediately and did not remember her dreams.

With wisps of hay littering her mussed hair, Lizzie giggled as she buttoned up her blouse. She playfully pushed the stableboy away from her. On her flushed face was a self-satisfied smile. Josh was a bit young, but he was just what she needed to satisfy her sexual appetite. If the master ever found out she would be dismissed without references, but that danger made sex all the more exciting.

"I've got to get to work," she said impatiently and pushed him away again. "The Lady Cassandra will be wantin' 'er 'ot cocoa fer the night."

"Wot would yer say if I told yer a secret about

the mistress?" her companion asked. "Would yer come back tonight?"

Lizzie looked at him with renewed interest. "A secret, eh? Well, maybe I could come fer a little while, if it's good wot yer 'ave to tell."

Josh smiled and pulled playfully on the pale blue satin ribbon laced through her blouse. Lizzie pushed him away, but not before he had undone the ribbon.

"Don't yer wanna 'ear me secret?" he teased, dangling his prize just out of her reach.

"Well, come on, out wit it," she demanded, trying to wrestle the blue satin from his hand.

"I saw the mistress tonight 'ave a secret meetin' wit that strange girl wot used to work 'ere. The one in men's breeches."

Ah ha, Lizzie thought, feeling powerful with this new knowledge. "That *is* good," she said. Pleased with himself, the stableboy leaned toward her for a kiss. Lizzie snatched her ribbon from his grasp and jumped up.

"I just might come by tonight," she said haughtily, "and I might not . . ."

The stableboy lay back into the hay and fondled himself suggestively. "Yer'll be back," he smirked.

Lizzie whirled away from him and hurried to the manor house. She knew this tidbit of information would be worth something to the master. She'd finally get back at her snippy little mistress. It was just a matter of picking the right time to tell . . .

CHAPTER 5

Soon after Alex left, Lord Alfred paid a call on Lord Stonehurst. The two remained closeted in Lord Stonehurst's library for many hours. Lady Cassandra was unaware of his visit until Lizzie mentioned it, more to see what her mistress's reaction would be than from any desire to provide information.

Cassandra sat at her dressing table and closed her eyes. Lizzie was more clumsy than usual today. Her rough hands had pulled Cassandra's blonde curls more than once. Putting the last finishing touches on the simple hair style, Lizzie took a deep breath.

"That 'andsome Lord Alfred were 'ere t'day, visitin' yer papa, 'e were."

Cassandra's eyes flew open and she started. In the mirror, her eyes flashed with fear and her cheeks reddened with ire. "What did he want?" she demanded.

"I don't really know," Lizzie answered. "I only just saw 'im go wit yer papa into the library."

Cassandra dismissed Lizzie with a wave of her hand. With a quick curtsy, the maid left her to her troubled thoughts. She wondered what the odious Lord Alfred wanted. Perhaps they were negotiating the purchase of something, a horse perhaps. She decided against asking her parents about the visit. The less she mentioned his name, the less they would think of him as a potential son-in-law.

A quiet week passed before Lady Cassandra was suddenly called into her papa's library again. She was completely unprepared for the fury she saw in his eyes. His frowning, red face caused her stomach to knot, and she nervously brushed a wisp of hair off her forehead. She began to play with the dotted calico overskirt of her gown as he paced back and forth without saying a word. Suddenly, he whirled to face her and spoke through clenched teeth.

"You deliberately defied me and saw that creature Alex again. I forbade you to see her. I ordered her gone before sundown, but you two had a secret meeting. Don't bother to deny it. I have shown you more tolerance than any of my peers would show their daughters, and this is what you do in return? I will not tolerate such disobedience. You will marry Lord Alfred within the month. He has agreed to the marriage despite your behavior at our ball."

She stood in speechless shock, panic welling up inside her, making it difficult to breathe. Dear God! It couldn't be true what she was hearing. She took in great gulps of air as she struggled to keep from swooning. She grasped the edge of the big wooden desk and swayed. Her papa saw her discomfort and came over to grab hold of her arms and lower her into a chair. However, the stubborn determination in his face did not change.

"I am sorry my decision distresses you so," he said as he burnt some feathers and then held them under her nose, a service he performed more for her mother than for her. The harsh scent cleared Cassandra's head immediately. "You'll find marriage to Lord Alfred not such a bad thing. He is handsome and young and strong. You'll have healthy, beautiful children."

Cassandra shook her head. "Do you think beautiful children and a handsome husband is all it takes to make me happy? Don't you know me at all? I don't want to marry anyone, least of all that odious man you find so suitable. He is a rake and a scoundrel."

"I knew that creature had influenced you, but I didn't realize how much. We are marrying you off just in time." His voice softened. "A young woman your age doesn't know what she wants. It is up to us, your parents, to do what is best. As for Lord Alfred's shortcomings, well ... he is a man. It is expected that he gain experience before he marries.

Your mother will talk to you about this." He paused before continuing with some embarrassment. "I'm aware that some people harbor what I consider unnatural feelings for their own sex, but that you, my own daughter, should be caught up in such things is unthinkable. Perhaps you were bored, or I've been too permissive with you. By eighteen a woman should already be married, with a child on the way. Your mother was but seventeen when you were born. Because the birth was very difficult, she could never have more children. I've never regretted that."

Cassandra tilted her head to look up at him. "Papa, you have always been so good to me," she pleaded. "Don't force this marriage, please. Send me away for a while. I just need time to think about it."

"The subject is closed. Go to your room, Cassandra. I'll have Lizzie bring you something cool to drink."

He turned his back on her and sat behind his desk. Cassandra stood and walked stiffly out the door, her thoughts racing as she wondered if her mother would be any help in dissuading her papa from his purpose. She thought not. Learning the identity of the person who had betrayed her was her first goal. Her logical choice was James or perhaps a stableboy, but she couldn't recall having seen anyone in the stables the night Alex left.

The first thing she did was write a letter to Alex in care of Aunt Sophia. If she guessed correctly, Alex would be arriving there any day now. It was important to let her know the turn of events and ask her to return to Stonehurst Manor to help her escape. When Lizzie arrived with a tray laden with

the promised cool drink and some small watercress sandwiches, Cassandra gave her the letter with orders to post it forthwith. Lizzie set down the tray and pocketed the letter, a smug smile on her face.
"You *will* post my letter?" Lady Cassandra asked sternly.
"Why yes, milady," Lizzie replied sweetly.
The self-satisfied smirk on the maid's face engendered a terrible suspicion in Cassandra's mind. As Lizzie turned to leave, Cassandra beckoned her to stay.
"Lizzie, do you have a beau?" she asked with studied casualness.
Startled, Lizzie answered quickly. "Well, yes. I see the stableboy, Josh, at times. Not often though."
"It must be hard to find time to be together. You both have many duties. Where do you meet?"
The maid was wary now. "Dif'rent places."
"In the stables?" Cassandra prompted.
"Sometimes."
"Yes, well, I was just interested. I hope you'll find your special beau soon. You may go now."
Cassandra contemplated this new information. So Josh had been there that night. She knew Lizzie would take any opportunity to raise her status in the household, and she knew the maid had no loyalty to her. It would be too suspicious if she suddenly asked for a real lady's maid, so she resolved to be very careful in the future. Ruefully, she thought of the letter to Alex she had delivered into Lizzie's hands and could only hope it would be posted.

* * * * *

Lizzie quickly left the bedroom. She thought the mistress was acting very strangely, and she wondered if she had been too forthcoming, if Lady Cassandra would guess that Josh had been in the stables that night.

Well, the mistress didn't know that Lord Stonehurst had given orders that any letters to or from Lady Cassandra were to be intercepted. It wouldn't be long now before Lizzie's status in the household rose, once the master rewarded her for her loyalty. He might even make her an upstairs maid.

Once downstairs, she handed the letter to the butler, who in turn gave it to the earl. She asked the butler later what had happened.

"Right into the fire," he answered. "Didn't read it or even look at the address."

The banns for the marriage of Lady Cassandra and Lord Alfred were announced. The ceremony would take place November 15 at Stonehurst Manor in three short weeks. It had been a little more than three months since her debut. Lady Cassandra's time became occupied with the ordering of her trousseau and wedding gown. With the wedding so close, the seamstresses worked practically day and night. Lady Elinor was very excited about the wedding; nothing was too good for her only daughter. Cassandra long ago had given up the idea of appealing to her mother, who would never go against her husband's wishes. She didn't know that her mother had succeeded in getting Lord Stonehurst to agree not to force his daughter to see Lord Alfred before the prenuptial dinner the night before the wedding.

Although she had vowed that this wedding would never take place, Cassandra pretended to be drawn into the excitement of ordering new clothes. She found it ironic that, under different circumstances, she would have loved the wedding gown. It was the epitome of the latest regency fashion. The bodice and underskirt were cut from soft, creamy white silk. Seed pearls and tiny glittering rubies encrusted the frothy lace overskirt. The long sleeves began with a small puff at the shoulders and ended at the wrist. A modest edging of lace lined the low-cut, square neckline. The sheer bridal veil was layered so that her face would barely be seen until the time came for the new husband to kiss his bride.

The last fitting took place a few days before the wedding. After the final stitch was in place and the seamstress had taken her leave, Cassandra sat alone and sighed. She knew she would never wear the beautiful gown, or anything like it, once she joined Alex. Although there had been no word from her, she planned to hire herself out as a lady's companion while Alex worked as a laborer, and she hoped they would have enough to live on. She did not fool herself into thinking her parents would ever forgive her, but she did wonder if Aunt Sophia would help them. After all, her aunt had never married and she lived a comfortable life.

Cassandra stepped carefully among the many yards of material draped throughout her bedroom and absently fingered the expensive lace. She picked up one finished gown after another, admiring the fine handiwork and wishing she had given more effort to her sewing lessons. They had seemed so useless at the time, but now that she considered working to support herself, the lessons were invaluable.

As she picked up yet another gem-encrusted gown, she suddenly realized that she held in her fingers a means of obtaining money. She hadn't planned on packing many clothes, but she knew the lace and gems on some of the gowns would fetch a good price. She didn't think one or two dresses would be missed out of the many. She choose the most expensive and hid them in her armoire, along with some other small valuables she had been collecting.

Pacing, she wondered why she hadn't heard from Alex. The wedding was only a few days away, and she'd counted on Alex coming to her aid. Yes, she could get away from the manor house easily enough, but she had no experience on the roads. There was no telling what could befall a gently bred young woman out on her own and unchaperoned.

She didn't want to think that Alex had forgotten her. This waiting made her feel almost desperate. Cassandra sat down again and put her head in her hands. She missed Alex more intensely with every day that passed. Just thinking of the way Alex touched her made her tremble. She missed the horsey, clean scent of her, and being surrounded by her strong arms. And yes, she missed seeing Alex in the tight breeches that showed off every feminine curve, and the loose shirts that gave enticing glimpses of softly rounded breasts. In a fit of pique, Cassandra hurled a pair of newly made shoes across the room. They landed with a satisfying thud. Lizzie threw open the door with a startled gasp. She carried a tray in her hands.

"Ooh mistress, wot is wrong?" she exclaimed as she set the tray down on a table. "I 'eard such a bangin'."

"Everything is fine Lizzie," Cassandra answered brusquely. She should never have trusted the maid, and wished she could have her dismissed. "Tell me, have I received any letters today?"

"Why no, milady. Yer 'ave not got any letters from that girl since she left."

Cassandra looked at her sharply. "What makes you think I am expecting letters from her? What have you been doing with my letters?"

Lizzie backed away toward the door when she recognized Cassie's blazing anger. "Nothin', I swear. 'Tis not me wot checks the post."

"Get out. I don't want to see you again. I will have you dismissed if you come near me again. Go and spread your poison elsewhere."

Cassandra undressed herself, struggling with rows of buttons and complicated lacings. Her wedding day nightmare was approaching quickly, and she was finally at a loss of what to do. She wished for the first time that she had not been born into the nobility.

Alex had arrived safely at Dovecote and was welcomed with open arms. Once the exhausted traveler was well-fed and rested, Cassandra's aunt put Alex to work in the neglected garden. A strong, independent spirit who had herself, as a young woman, developed a romantic, special friendship for a lady friend, Sophia immediately recognized Alex for what she was.

Sophia had chosen to live the life of a spinster rather than marry, but a small inheritance made that possible. The woman she had loved had given up what she considered a childish infatuation and had married, like any dutiful daughter was expected to do. The two women didn't keep in touch, but Sophia knew everything about her friend's life, and when the woman died giving birth to her sixth child, Sophia was saddened. It suited her to live isolated in the country with no one but her loyal servants. She liked to be surrounded by cheerful young women. When Alex arrived with a letter from her niece, Sophia quickly discerned the situation and invited Alex to stay. She even insisted that Alex call her "Aunt Sophia."

When Sophia received a wedding invitation from her brother, she refrained from telling Alex. Perhaps she had been wrong about the two women, she mused silently as she reread her brother's letter. Or perhaps Cassandra was like Sophia's first love? There was nothing to indicate anything other than a normal betrothal and wedding, although it did seem rather hasty. Could Lady Cassandra have gotten herself with child?

A few days later Sophia resolved to tell Alex and see her reaction before deciding whether to attend. A trip to Stonehurst Manor was never an easy undertaking, and giving herself merely a fortnight to get there merely made the trip more strenuous. She wrapped a white cashmere shawl around her slim shoulders and strolled into the garden. Alex was kneeling in the dirt, weeding Aunt Sophia's beloved roses. Sophia watched silently for a few moments, enjoying the slight rippling of the muscles in Alex's arms as she dug deeply into the moist earth. Alex sensed her presence and looked up with a warm smile.

Sophia reached out and lightly touched Alex's chestnut hair. "I've come to depend on you already, Alex. I don't think I could part with you now."

Alex stood and brushed the dirt from her legs. "I love it here, Aunt Sophia. It will be wonderful when Cassie arrives. You will help us, won't you?"

"Alex," she began gently, "how can you be sure Cassandra will come? Maybe she just wanted to give you a place to stay after my brother dismissed you."

"Oh no, Aunt Sophia. Cassie loves me. She promised to come."

Sophia smiled at Alex's openness and innocence. Most women would not talk so carelessly of their love for another woman. She was glad that Alex felt safe with her, but knew the young woman would have to learn discretion, as she had. She might appear frail, but the frailty was an illusion. In spirit, Sophia was very strong and determined. It wasn't easy as an unmarried woman to survive in a man's world, but at least she didn't have to live the life of so many women who weren't born into money.

Sophia tilted her head to look up at the tall woman. She searched Alex's golden-brown eyes and knew what she was about to tell her would cause great pain. She ran her fingers through her graying hair and took a deep breath.

"Cassandra won't be coming here, Alex." Sophia watched her intently. "She is getting married in a fortnight."

Alex's eyes widened in surprise. "No, you must be mistaken. She has plans to come here. We love each other. Who would she marry?"

Sophia silently handed her the wedding invitation. Alex read it in disbelief. Her eyes filled with loathing when she saw Lord Alfred's name.

"This can't be true!" she exploded. "Cassie hates that man. If she is marrying him, it's against her will. That must be why she hasn't written. I must go to her!" Alex's face was twisted in torment.

Sophia lay her hand on the young woman's arm and felt the trembling of her rage. "I'm very sorry, Alex," she said comfortingly, "but I don't think it is a good idea for you to go there. Young women change. I know what you must be feeling. It is likely that Cassandra realized that what you and she had was an infatuation, a novelty, no more."

Alex clenched and unclenched her fists. "No! You are wrong, and I am going to prove it to you. I will go to Stonehurst Manor and fetch her."

Sophia began to speak, but Alex stopped her. "I have the money Cassie gave me. I will hire a horse if you won't let me borrow one."

"Of course you may borrow a horse, Alex," Sophia began, "but don't you think . . ."

Alex didn't wait to hear the rest. The rose bushes forgotten, she turned on her heel and hurried into the house. Sophia tenderly touched one faded yellow rose and noted the brown edging on its petals. The coming of winter always depressed her. She slowly returned to the house. Alex was already gone. Sophia sat at her desk to write her brother and tell him she would be unable to attend the wedding.

CHAPTER 6

"Cassandra darling, you must snap out of this depression," Lady Stonehurst said as she entered her daughter's bedroom and saw the bride-to-be sitting forlornly on the window seat. "Your wedding is tomorrow, my love, and it will be beautiful. Soon you will forget the past, especially when you have children to care for. Children can help you forget many things."

Something in her mother's voice made Cassandra look up at her curiously. It never occurred to her that perhaps her mother might be unhappy. Now

Cassandra wondered if she, too, had suffered disappointment when she was young. Perhaps her mother had never wanted to marry Clayton Stonehurst. That girls and women had their lives dictated first by a father and then by a husband was so very unfair. They were treated as if they had no minds or wills of their own. Well, she for one was not going to be dictated to. She had a daring plan of escape, with or without Alex's help.

Ignoring her mother's presence, she turned her attention to the activities outside her window. Servants were setting up the garden for the wedding luncheon that would take place after the ceremony. There would be a ball later that evening. The weather was unseasonably mild. Cassandra spitefully hoped it would rain and ruin everything.

Lady Stonehurst began to look through her daughter's armoire. "Come, let me help you get ready for dinner," she cooed. "You'll be seeing your future husband for the first time since the betrothal, and you'll want to look your best."

Her concentration broken once again, Cassandra rose from the window seat. The thought of seeing Lord Alfred made her feel ill. Lady Stonehurst was removing an organdy evening gown of sunset yellow from the armoire, but Cassandra pushed past her and grabbed a plain gown of gray silk. It was stark in its simplicity and as close to a gown of mourning as anything she owned.

"That is a horrid gown, Cassandra," her mother protested. "It makes you look washed out. Please, you must look nice for Lord Alfred."

"Don't try to treat this situation as if it's something I want," Cassandra snapped. "I hate that man and I never wanted to marry him. You and Papa are making my life miserable."

"Why can't you just accept this?" her mother pleaded. "It will make everything easier for you. I understand how you feel." Her mother hesitated for a moment. "I ... I ... didn't want to marry your father either, but I have learned to love him. Give it time."

"No! I don't want to be like you. I don't need a husband."

"Don't be silly, child. Every woman needs a man to take care of her."

"Alex doesn't," Cassandra argued. "She says she'll never marry."

Her mother's face hardened, her mouth drawing into a thin line of determination. "Your father was right in sending that creature away. I won't tolerate this behavior, Cassandra. Now, get dressed. Dinner is at eight."

She tossed the yellow gown on the bed and left the room. As soon as the door closed, Cassandra flew into action. She had planned on waiting until everyone had gone to bed to make her escape, but she knew she couldn't sit through a dinner with the wretched Lord Alfred. She retrieved her carefully packed valise from the back of the armoire, and into it she stuffed a few pieces of jewelry. There would be no time to get food, but she had a few gold guineas left and would use them to buy dinner at a roadside inn. She dressed in her plainest gown, one of lightweight brown wool, almost spartan in its cut, and threw on a black woolen cloak with a concealing hood. She needed to look as inconspicuous as possible. Carefully opening her bedroom door, she peeked cautiously into the hallway. No one was about. They were probably getting ready for the prenuptial dinner. She crept down the stairs undetected.

Cassandra slipped through the drawing room doors and sped across the lawn to the stables. She went to Appleton's stall, and he neighed in welcome. She hated to leave her precious stallion behind, but he was too magnificent an animal for a single, unchaperoned woman to own. Highwaymen would surely set upon her to steal him. Instead, she would take her papa's older, more gentle horse, Blue Mist. Cassandra felt the tears well in her eyes as Appleton nuzzled her in search of an apple.

"Appleton," she whispered, "I am going to miss you so much. I hope you won't miss me. Maybe one day I can come back and fetch you."

She stroked his soft nose for several minutes before pulling away. Hurrying toward Blue Mist's stall, she knew she had wasted precious time. At any moment James or a stableboy might discover her. She adjusted the bridle, quickly threw a saddle over Blue Mist's back, and fastened it tightly, thankful for all that Alex had taught her. Tossing one last look back at Appleton, she urged Blue Mist out of the stable at a sedate walk. She kept close to the trees as she traveled the gravel driveway, praying all the while that she wouldn't meet anyone coming to the manor house for dinner. Once on the public road she spurred the horse into a brisk canter. The sunset was a glorious blaze of red orange and golden yellow as Cassandra left the estate grounds behind and headed north. The fleeing heiress would not be able to rest for hours; she needed to put many miles between herself and Stonehurst Manor before her parents discovered she was missing.

The sunset gave way to an unusually clear night lit by a bright full moon. Cassandra felt it was both a blessing and a curse — the moon would light her way, but clouds would have afforded her the cover of darkness. She could only hope that no one would take note of her.

At the very same time, trying to keep out of sight by taking side roads, Alex was traveling south. Keeping off the main roads had made the normal ten-day journey stretch into thirteen. Having practically run Aunt Sophia's horse to death, she spurred him into yet another exhausted run, vowing to make it up to the poor creature somehow. Alex and Lady Cassandra unknowingly passed each other on different roads. Being in a single-minded hurry to get to Cassie, it is doubtful she would have noticed the darkly garbed horsewoman anyway.

As breathless as her horse, Alex arrived near Stonehurst just as the alarm was sounded that Lady Cassandra had disappeared. Unaware of this event, Alex stopped in Fulbourn until she could devise a plan to see Lady Cassandra. She was standing in the road in front of the village's disreputable Hound's Tooth Inn when the thunder of horses attracted her attention. It was the search party from Stonehurst Manor. Silhouetted in the light spilling from the inn, her woman's form in its tight-fitting men's clothes must have been unmistakable. One rider reined up next to her, his leering look raking her from head to toe. She saw that he rode Appleton.

"Well," Lord Alfred sneered, "if it isn't our insolent Alex. And what brings you here tonight, my dear?"

She backed away from him. He had the advantage, and she wanted to get into the relative safety of the inn. Purposefully, Lord Alfred quickly moved Appleton to block her way, then leapt down and grabbed her arms painfully. She jerked, trying to wrench his hands from her, but he held tightly as he pushed her into the darkness of the alley. His intent was clear in the wicked lechery in his eyes. Despite her unusual strength, she was no match for the man. He pushed her farther back into the alley while she struggled. She couldn't maneuver into an advantageous position.

"It's time you learned a lesson," he snarled, "and I am just the man to teach you. Let's see what you have under these breeches."

As Lord Alfred brutally tried to kiss her, a rat scrabbling in the slop-laden alley distracted him for a split second. He turned his head and his grip loosened slightly. Alex brought her knee smashing into Lord Alfred's groin. With a pained oath, he let go of her arms. She brought her fist back and then dealt him a crashing blow to the chin. He reeled backward, clutching his groin and moaning loudly. Finally, he fell to the ground and Alex gave him a swift, hard kick in the ribs as she hurried past his writhing form. Victory, she thought, smiling.

"That's for all the maids who couldn't fight you off, *Lord* Alfred," she hissed.

The confusion and noise outside the inn made it impossible for anyone to hear Lord Alfred's feeble cries for help. Alex knew he would be in a murderous rage once the pain she'd inflicted had abated. She didn't linger, but hurried to find her horse. Hearing Lady Cassandra's name made her pause.

"Where do yer s'pose the Lady Cassandra got off to?" a grizzled groom asked one of the younger members of the search party. "I 'ope we won't be out all bloody night long."

"Eh, she prob'ly traveled south. The master thinks she might be off to London. 'ow far can a girl get all alone, e'en if she do 'ave ol' Blue Mist?"

Alex didn't wait to hear more. Cursing her decision to travel the side roads, she ran to her horse. If only she'd been more willing to chance discovery, she would have met her beloved on the road! As she was about to mount her exhausted steed, Appleton caught her eye. The woman did not hesitate. She grabbed the saddlebag from her own horse and ran to Cassie's stallion. Seizing his reins, she flung her long legs over his broad back and galloped away. How far a head start Cassie had, Alex couldn't guess, but she was determined to find her, even if she had to ride all night. The thought of Lady Cassandra on the road alone in the dark sent Alex into a panic. The lovable fool didn't know the peril she was in!

* * * * *

Blissfully unaware that she had missed Alex, Cassandra kept Blue Mist at a steady canter. She didn't know how far she should travel to be safe, but decided to push Blue Mist until he was too tired to go farther. She would sleep wherever that happened to be.

It was exciting to be out on her own for the first time. Riding through the estate just wasn't the same thing. This was so much more adventurous. That her parents were worried and had probably sent out a search party didn't concern her. She was going to see Alex! And she wouldn't be marrying Lord Alfred in the morning. The thought of the man's touch made her shudder with horror. She threw her hood off and unpinned her hair so it streamed behind her. The night was exhilarating.

Cassandra allowed her horse to slow down. She didn't feel tired yet, but wanted to avoid the risk of hurting Blue Mist. She glanced behind her nervously, but no one was there. She was far from Fulbourn and Stonehurst Manor. No farmers' huts dotted the landscape. She finally felt safe.

A few miles behind, Alex sent Appleton into a run. She was in an uncharacteristic panic. The tension in her broad shoulders would make it evident to anyone who knew her, the scowl on her face to anyone who did not. The wind flowed through her loose shirt and whipped her cloak behind her, causing them to billow like the sails on a ship. Her short hair ruffled, tickling her scalp and making her feel wild and untamed.

Appleton's body heaved as she clenched the reins and dug her heels into his sides. His hooves seemed to fly as he poured all his strength into his stride. Alex became aware of something bumping her leg and reached back to find it was Lord Alfred's saddlebag. Barely slowing down, she reached inside. Her exploring fingers closed around the man's revolver. She smiled at her stroke of luck and urged Appleton onward. Her eyes scanned the darkness, looking for any sign of motion. Suddenly, a melee of shadowy figures loomed in the distance. Alex reined Appleton hard, causing him to rear up on his hind legs.

The hairs on the nape of her neck prickled as Cassandra sensed that she was no longer alone. She gripped the reins tightly, feeling her nails bite into her palms even through her gloves. Her eyes darted to the trees ahead. She felt the sweat break out on her upper lip. Her eyes strained, searching.

Unexpectedly, the shadows came alive, slithering out of the trees to become men on horseback. She gasped and kicked Blue Mist as hard as she could. She knew that with his superior breeding they could quickly outdistance any nags the men were riding. With her pulse beating wildly, she guided Blue Mist off the path, praying she could keep her precarious hold in the sidesaddle. The men raced to meet her, cutting off her escape just past the trees. Intent, they circled like wolves after a deer. Terrified, she felt the scream well up in her throat.

Quietly heading into the shelter of the trees, Alex strained to see what was happening. The figures on horseback were deliberately circling something, but she couldn't make out what it was. She was sure she had happened upon a band of highwaymen. A shrill scream cut through the night. Alex swore as she saw Lady Cassandra's horse rear up, thus revealing the object of the brigands' interest. Without a second thought, Alex kicked Appleton into a gallop and thundered into the confused band of men. She managed to snatch the revolver out of the saddlebag and fire it once into the air. Alex's heart beat wildly as she saw the flash of a knife in the moonlight. While one of the men held Blue Mist's reins, another was trying to cut through the girth on Cassandra's saddle. Alex fired again, satisfied to see one of the highwaymen jerk as he was hit. He fell to the ground, his horse galloping away.

Cassandra was trying to calm her horse, as well as herself. She kicked out as the man with the knife tried to catch her. He groaned and swore as her booted foot connected with his shin. Another shot rang out and another highwayman fell. She looked to her left, hoping to see a rescuer — even Lord Alfred would be welcome now — and not a rival brigand.

Someone grabbed her horse's reins, jerking them out of her hands. Her heart pounded. She sucked air into her lungs and kicked out blindly.

"Cassie! Cassie!" a familiar voice shouted above the din. "Don't fight me. Run! Please run!"

She clung to Blue Mist's mane as the two horses sped through the night, side by side. Somehow she had lost the reins. With perspiration and tears nearly blinding her, she concentrated on getting far away from the band of brigands. Gasping for air, she dared to glance over at the woman racing beside her — Alex! Tears of relief flowed freely as she recognized her strong features. And Appleton! How on earth had they found her?

Several miles later Alex swerved off the road and sped across an abandoned field to take shelter in an apple orchard. She was sure the highwaymen hadn't followed them. She brought the horses skidding to a halt. Lady Cassandra's hold on Blue Mist's mane loosened. Horrified, Alex watched as she slid from his back and fainted. Alex leapt off Appleton and knelt beside the unconscious woman.

Gently gathering her beloved into arms that ached, Alex kissed her forehead and then her nose. Alex felt eyelashes fluttering against her cheeks and raised her head to smile down at her. Deep blue eyes, red-rimmed from exhaustion and tears, twinkled back at her. With a sigh, Cassandra lifted her hand to pull Alex's head down. The women kissed tenderly, almost shyly, at first. Then Alex tightened her hold and their kiss deepened.

Cassandra's hands clasped Alex's head, her fingers moving sensuously through sweat-dampened hair.

"Ah, Alex, is it really you?" Cassandra murmured into her ear, her voice breaking.

"Yes, my beloved, 'tis I. I was frightened when I saw you surrounded by those men. I could only think of getting you away."

"My knight in shining armor." Lady Cassandra laughed. She glanced over to where the horses stood. "And on the mightiest of steeds."

"I have a good story for you," Alex began, but Cassandra quieted her with a kiss full of longing and pent-up passion.

In the darkness, with only the nocturnal creatures to see and hear them, Alex and Cassandra made up for the time they had been apart. Cassie's black cloak became their bed as they slowly undressed. Their skin glowed whitely in the night shadows. They shivered in the chilly November air. Alex pulled a fine linen shirt out of Lord Alfred's saddlebag and used it to wipe their hands and faces.

The lovers allowed their fingers to explore each other's bodies, enjoying the softness and, ultimately, the wetness. Cassandra lay across Alex, breast to breast, rubbing her leg up and down Alex's thigh. She alternately bit and licked Alex's sensitive neck. Her nipping teeth brought answering growls from Alex, who suddenly pushed Lady Cassandra onto her back and loomed above her.

"You have sharp little teeth," Alex said huskily, and then swooped down to kiss Cassie with the urgency of her need.

Lady Cassandra drew her nails lightly down Alex's back, making her shiver. Trailing teasing kisses across her throat and shoulders, Alex brought her lips slowly to Cassie's swollen breasts. Her back arched as Alex sucked a puckered nipple into her mouth. Her hands clutched the strong arms that held her. Alex's hand moved over Cassandra's belly, hesitating only momentarily as it hovered over the curling, damp hair that nestled between Cassandra's twitching legs. She probed gently with her fingers, urging Cassie to open herself. With an involuntary moan, Cassie spread her legs wider, thrusting her hips upward to take Alex's fingers into her. Alex smothered further moans with her kisses. She moved her fingers in and out of Cassandra's moist crevices, fluttering them as they passed over the place that made Cassandra writhe with pleasure.

As Alex continued her exploration of soft, wet folds, she continued to kiss first Cassie's lush mouth and then her heaving breasts. She licked the salty sweat from her smooth skin. Her own breathing quickened, and she could feel the thump of both their hearts.

Cassandra sucked in her breath as Alex's fingers increased their intensity and motion. She couldn't stop the shuddering of her limbs or tension in her muscles as her body prepared for blissful release. She opened her eyes and cried, "Alex!" The midnight sky spun in a dizzying swirl of flashing light. An explosion of stars overhead mirrored the explosion of her own climax.

Her body convulsing, Cassandra struggled to regain her breath. Alex held her and continued to caress her softly, without pressure. Alex's short hair tickled like wisps of straw. Cassandra took her eyes off the sky and stared into the golden-brown gaze of the woman she loved. The heaving of her chest slowed as her pounding heart quieted and her lungs drew in deep breaths of the cool night air.

Alex lay her head upon Cassie's shoulder and wrapped her arms tightly around her. She pulled her cloak over them and hushed Cassandra, who struggled against the desire for sleep in favor of bringing the same pleasure to Alex.

"Sleep, my love," Alex whispered, "we have plenty of time ahead of us. We cannot stay here long for Lord Alfred will be looking for me, for us. Hush now. Sleep."

Alex felt Cassandra's body go limp. She carefully changed position so she was on her back and brought Cassie's head to rest upon her breast. She didn't mind the dried, prickly grass or fallen twigs poking through Cassandra's cloak. She breathed in the pungent odor of their lovemaking, mingled with the earthy odor of moldering leaves and damp soil. She registered the sounds of the night — the soft jingling of their horse's reins, an owl's whispering wings, the rustling of remnant leaves in the trees. Somewhere, a small brook splashed and gurgled. Pressing her lover close, Alex fell into an exhausted sleep.

CHAPTER 7

Lord Alfred writhed on the debris-laden ground in the malodorous alleyway next to the Hound's Tooth Inn. He struggled to control his moans of pain as he clutched his throbbing groin. Cursing the cross-dressing stablemaid and vowing revenge, he finally managed to stand on shaky legs and hobble to the alley's entrance. The cobblestoned street was a mass of confusion. Men and horses milled about aimlessly as raucous laughter spilled from the brightly lit doorway of the inn. As Lord Alfred sagged against a stone wall, a member of the search party called to him.

"Well, guv'nor," the Stonehurst Manor stablehand snickered, "looks like yer done searchin' fer a time. Some ruffian done take yer 'orse, and if yer don' mind me saying so, yer ain't lookin' too good any'ow."

"You insolent boy!" He was appalled at the break in his voice. "Find Lord Stonehurst immediately, and tell him I've been set upon by highwaymen."

The stablehand stared at him as if to question, highwaymen? None in their right mind would have attacked him here, especially with so many people about. Their method was surprise on a deserted stretch of road. He didn't care. If he said he'd been attacked, then so be it. It was not in the stablehand's best interests to argue.

Lord Alfred retreated into the darkness of the alley. There was no way he would admit that a mere woman had incapacitated him. He ripped his purse, leaving its leather strings hanging and torn, stuffed the moneybag under his shirt, then scraped his gleaming Hessian boots against the rough stone wall to further mar and scratch their immaculate surface. His clothes were already dirty and smelly from his fall. Hiding his face in the shadows, the scheming nobleman punched himself in the eye as hard as he could, hoping it would blacken. Grimacing in pain but satisfied now that his scruffed-up appearance would corroborate his lie, he stepped into the street and headed for the doorway of the inn.

The tavern was loud and bright, and the stench of dirty bodies and spilled food and drink made it smell worse than a stable. Lord Alfred, however, being a frequent visitor of such establishments, was not bothered by the noise or odor. His own disheveled appearance fit right in with the other revelers. He pushed his way through the throng of drunken men and found a scarred wooden chair. A comely barmaid was at his side almost immediately, and he ordered a pint of stout.

The serving wench returned quickly with his drink. He drank it down and ordered another. For the moment, Lord Alfred forgot about Alex and began to wonder what to do next. He knew that he should borrow another horse and rejoin the search party, but he had no intention of doing so. Lord Alfred had tired of the excitement of the chase, and just wanted to nurse his wounded pride as a jilted suitor. Besides, the soreness between his legs reminded him that he wouldn't want to be on a horse just now anyway.

Alfred drank his second pint and thoughtfully rubbed his chin. Clayton Stonehurst would be most anxious to marry his daughter off now, he mused. He might even be persuaded to increase her dowry. After all, who would marry a hellion such as she? Lord Alfred knew he would have to approach this matter very carefully, so as not to appear too greedy. Right now, however, he would enjoy his ale and the very friendly serving wench. He snapped his fingers and she hurried over again.

It was many hours and many pints later that Lord Alfred noticed his future father-in-law standing at the doorway of the tavern. Lord Stonehurst wrinkled his nose in distaste as he surveyed the room. One of the revelers pointed him to Lord

Alfred's table. Wincing in pain, he made his way through the crowd. It was then that Lord Alfred noticed that the earl was limping badly.

"My God, man!" Clayton exclaimed, as he approached Lord Alfred's table. "I was told you had been set upon by highwaymen, but I could not believe it. They attacked you here? In the alley?"

Lord Alfred moaned and rubbed his swollen eye. "Those bastards get more brazen every day. They got my money and my horse." He held up his frayed purse strings as evidence, hoping his voice wasn't a bit too loud or his gestures too dramatic.

"I couldn't imagine why you hadn't joined us," Stonehurst began, watching the young lord suspiciously. "Are you badly injured?"

Alfred knew he was under scrutiny. "But what of you?" he asked, hoping to change the subject. "Are you hurt as well?"

"I had a rather nasty fall," Lord Stonehurst replied, favoring his left leg as he sat. "That blasted stableboy didn't tighten my saddle properly, and I was too hurried to check it myself when I mounted. Damned thing came loose in full gallop. I nearly broke my leg when I hit the ground. Only God saved me from being trampled by the others."

"Well then, let us drink to misfortune," Alfred said wryly, handing his injured companion his pint of stout, and signaling to the barmaid to bring two more.

Clayton ignored the gesture. "I've sent the search party on ahead," he continued. "We can only pray that Cassandra is not found first by the highwaymen who attacked you."

Lord Alfred had stopped listening. With a gulp of

ale, he turned to Lord Stonehurst to play the outraged bridegroom. "Sir," he began, "your daughter has shown an unfeminine propensity for disobedience. I am humiliated. What are you prepared to do?"

"What do you mean? We will find her and she will marry you. It is settled."

The serving wench arrived with more ale. "Something more, milord?" she asked suggestively as she sidled up against Lord Alfred. As his hand snaked around to squeeze her plump ass, she leaned forward to allow him and his companion a good look at her overflowing decolletage. Her tangled auburn hair tickled his cheek.

"Another round, lass," Lord Alfred replied, "and something to eat." She scooted away. He knew her eagerness to please was because she hoped he'd be generous with his money.

Lord Alfred turned to Lord Stonehurst. "I don't know if the affair is settled, my lord." His voice was beginning to slur from too much drink. "Your daughter is no longer beyond reproach. She is traveling alone, at night. Her reputation is compromised."

"We have an agreement, you and I," Lord Stonehurst replied through clenched teeth. "Cassandra is young and headstrong, that is all. She will be a good wife and mother. You know that she is a virtuous woman."

Alfred gave a disdainful sniff. "Virtuous? I was marrying her under less than desirable circumstances to begin with. After all, she has treated me very rudely, not at all like a bride should treat her husband-to-be. People will talk behind my back. And now, there is no telling what is happening with Lady Cassandra."

"Are you telling me that you don't intend to marry my daughter?"

Lord Alfred finished his ale and motioned to the auburn-haired barmaid for yet another round. He concentrated his attention on his manicured nails and said casually, "She would be considered damaged merchandise by most men. However, with a small increase in her dowry, I shall be prepared to honor the marriage contract."

Lord Stonehurst stood up abruptly. "I think you overstep the bounds of decent behavior, Lord Alfred," he said angrily. "Your insinuations are an insult. We must rise early tomorrow to continue the search for Cassandra. Do you not think you should return home with me?"

Lord Alfred watched the comely serving wench returning with his order. She had a very sensuous sway to her hips and he licked his lips. He knew he would not sleep alone that night. He smiled to himself and looked up at the other man. "You go on, my lord," he said. "I will see you in the morning."

"Very well," the earl answered stonily as he turned on his heel.

At the door, he looked back to see Lord Alfred pull the serving wench onto his lap. The man's hand was already inside her ruffled blouse, and she was nibbling his ear. Disgusted by Alfred's behavior, he decided then that he would never hold his daughter to such a marriage contract. She was right. Lord

Alfred was a scoundrel, and certainly not someone who should take control of Stonehurst Manor.

As he climbed wearily onto his horse, he worried and wondered about his daughter. Where could she be? Was she safe? He would never forgive himself for forcing her to flee. Had he known that Cassandra was with Alex, he would have been both relieved and annoyed, for as much as he disliked Alex, Cassie's safety was more important.

The night passed uneventfully for the two women. As the sun peeked over the hills, Alex woke and smiled at the sleeping face of her beloved. She hated to wake her, but they had many days of travel before they would reach Dovecote. Alex assumed Lord Alfred would tell everyone that he had seen her, and the searchers would, in turn, assume that Lady Cassandra was with her. For safety, they would travel the long route across farm fields, rather than along public roads.

Although the morning was chill, Alex could tell from the clear sky that they would have another mild day. The mist that had crept in after midnight left only remnants of moisture on the vegetation. The sweet odor of rotting apples on the ground around them made her stomach growl.

Alex sat up, letting the cloak fall off her shoulders. Goose bumps rose on her bare skin. Cassandra was still sleeping innocently. Her vulnerable nakedness made Alex tremble with renewed desire, but she knew that it was dangerous to be in such a state now. Before she could lose her resolve, Alex dressed quickly, then lay down beside Cassandra again.

She shook the sleepinq woman gently. "Wake up, Cassie. We must head out early."

"Not now, Lizzie," Cassandra mumbled and threw out her arm. When her hand encountered Alex's breast, her eyes flew open in wide surprise. Recognition dawned, and she giggled. "You must congratulate me," she teased. "Today is my wedding day."

Alex frowned. "Don't even joke about that, Cassie. Come, your Aunt Sophia awaits us. You must get dressed and then we can find something to eat."

Cassandra sat up and embraced her. "Don't be so serious, my love. It is so wonderful to be with you again. I loved sleeping in your arms. I don't need food, only you."

Alex leaned down for a quick kiss before she untangled herself from Cassandra's arms and stood up. To Cassie, she looked strong and confident as she towered above her. She sighed and closed her eyes, then felt Alex's booted foot nudge her in response. Still playing, she refused to open her eyes, but stretched luxuriously to tease Alex with her nakedness.

Suddenly, several thumps near her ear startled her. She opened her eyes to see Alex a short distance away, carefully aiming hard, wrinkled apples. Cassandra sat up indignantly, tossing her head with intended aristocratic arrogance. As she stood to retrieve her gown and brush the dirt and grass from it, another apple caught her squarely on her naked backside. With an unladylike yelp, Cassie jerked upright, clutched the gown to her breast, and glared at the woman who was laughing at her.

"I don't find your behavior at all amusing," she complained with a haughty sniff. "I see that my aunt hasn't managed to turn you into a lady."

Alex's long legs quickly carried her over to where Cassandra stood. She grabbed Cassie's shoulders and shook her gently. "If I thought you meant what you've just said, I would leave you here to find your own way back."

Cassandra smiled and gently touched Alex's cheek. "You know I wouldn't want you to change one bit. Now, how about something to eat? These apples look edible."

Cassie slipped her clothes on and followed the sound of water to the brook. The water was low and therefore slightly clouded with silt, but she washed her hands and face as best she could and then rinsed her mouth with the water. It tasted good anyway, cold and refreshing.

The two lovers sat on the black cloak and fed each other. Alex had some day-old bread left over. The apples were hard and tangy. Cassandra's lips puckered, beckoning Alex to kiss her. They leaned forward at the same time, eyes closed and mouths parted. Their kiss was deep and apple-sweet. Alex gripped her arms, as if to push her back onto the cloak and make love to her right there, but Cassandra pushed her away and stood laughing. She held her hand out to Alex. Alex grabbed on, and it took all of Cassandra's strength not to topple over as she helped Alex rise.

"You must lose some weight," she said, giggling, and ran toward her stallion. Appleton stamped two hooves and snorted, as if delighted see her. "I can't believe you brought me my horse," Cassie exclaimed, caressing his soft nose. "How did you get him?"

Alex began to saddle Blue Mist. "I took him from Lord Alfred."

"Lord Alfred?" Cassandra asked with distaste. "I can't believe that man had the nerve to ride my horse." Suddenly she cried out in dismay. "Oh Alex! Look at this!"

Cassie held the leather band needed to fasten the sidesaddle. Alex gasped when she saw it and explained what had happened. The highwayman's knife had nearly achieved its purpose: the girth was practically cut in two!

"What can we do now?" Cassie moaned. "There's no way that this girth will hold. It is a miracle that it didn't break last night when we rode away."

Alex inspected the damage, then went and got the other saddle. "Well, love," she said, throwing the saddle onto Appleton's back, "I believe it's time you learned to ride astride."

"Astride?" Cassie gasped. "Why, even if I knew how, I certainly can't ride astride in this gown!"

Alex tightened the girth around Appleton's middle, then reached into her saddlebag and pulled out an old pair of breeches. Grinning broadly, she threw them at Cassandra. "I just got these from my dressmaker, milady. I believe they will go perfectly with your gown."

Cassandra leaned over and gingerly picked up the men's breeches. She blushed profusely at the mere thought of putting them on. Bunching her gown around her waist, she quickly pulled the breeches up her legs and over her hips. The rough material felt scratchy even through her pantalettes. Struggling with the buttons, Cassie looked over to see Alex smirking.

"Don't you dare laugh at me!" she ordered. "These are totally inappropriate for me."

Within moments, Alex's deft fingers had finished the task. The breeches slid halfway down over Cassandra's hips. Alex could contain her laughter no more.

Cassandra burned with anger as she pulled the breeches up. Then the humor of the situation caught her too. She could only imagine what she must look like. Her embarrassment evaporated like morning dew in the midday sun, and she laughed with Alex.

"I think you look wonderful," Alex chuckled. "You might start a new fashion." She strode over to her saddlebag and pulled out a thin rope. "Here, I think this might help."

Cassandra tied it around her waist. The breeches stayed up. She then lowered her gown over her legs. The dress completely covered the unfamiliar article of clothing.

"You'll have to hike the gown up again when you sit astride the horse, Cassie."

She did so, and then Alex lifted her onto the stallion's back. The feel of the saddle between her legs caused her to blush again. This adventure was certainly tearing down more than one convention. She squirmed uncomfortably in the saddle and frowned at the strange sensations. She imagined what Alex must be feeling with only a saddle blanket to separate her thighs from the horse's body.

"Are you ready?" Alex asked, watching her closely.

In reply, Cassandra took a deep breath, loosened her hold on the reins, and touched her heels to Appleton's side. He began walking slowly and Alex let Blue Mist follow.

They headed out of the trees. Cassandra watched the sun-bronzed Alex confidently riding Blue Mist. If it were possible for her to be even more muscular than Cassie remembered, she was indeed. Living with Aunt Sophia had been good for her. Alex looked stronger and healthier, and certainly more happy.

They crossed the small brook and came to an open field that had been planted over with alfalfa for the winter months. After carefully picking their way through the furrows, they followed a small dirt path that would wind around fields and villages practically all the way to Aunt Sophia's estate.

As she began to get the feel for riding astride, Cassandra wondered how she could have ridden sidesaddle for so many years. She realized now that the women's saddle was really very uncomfortable and not at all secure. Then she thought about how absurd she must look in her filthy gown and breeches, and laughed softly to herself.

Smiling at Alex, Cassandra prompted, "You still haven't told me how you took Appleton from Lord Alfred."

"Lord Alfred was part of the search party sent to find you."

"I want to know everything," she demanded. "I am glad you were here to rescue me from those highwaymen, but how?"

Alex obliged and told her the full story, from the time Aunt Sophia showed her the wedding invitation to Lord Alfred lying helpless in the alley. Cassandra was in fits of laughter. She could not remember the last time she had been so happy and at ease. She could just imagine the impeccable lord writhing in agony in the filth, and knew he deserved every tear in his imported shirt and every scratch on his shiny Hessians.

After a time they were quiet, content to ride silently in each other's company. They looked for all the world like two farmers on a journey. Cassandra's torn, yet unmistakably expensive gown was covered by the black cloak now dirty and littered with bits of leaves from their night in the woods. Her glorious blonde hair fell in a tangled, dusty cascade down her back, and certainly did not resemble the locks of a lady of quality. Alex sat tall upon her horse, looking from afar like a man with her short-cropped hair and men's clothing, but Cassandra could see the swell of her full breasts with each breath she took, the linen shirt she was wearing having fallen open where Lord Alfred had torn the buttons off.

Afraid of what Alex might do and wanting to protect her in any way she could, Sophia decided to travel to her brother's estate after all. Soon after Alex had left Dovecote, she packed some clothes and, taking only a footman and driver, left on her journey. They would stop only at night. The main roads to Stonehurst were long and rutted. The coach was not new, and its worn springs did little to ease the rocking or to cushion the jolts caused by each bump in the road. Sophia fretted as she bounced along, fearful of what might happen when Alex reached Stonehurst. She wished she had visited her brother and his family more often, then perhaps this whole mess could have been avoided. Surely she would have seen that her niece was different and more like herself. It probably wouldn't have mattered; her brother was very stubborn and disapproved of unwed females. Sophia was convinced he wouldn't have allowed his daughter and heir to mimic his spinster sister.

Finally, many days later, they reached Fulbourn. The coach slowed on its way through the village. Feeling a bit sick after being confined for so long, Sophia stuck her head out the window for some air. The noise coming from the Hound's Tooth Inn at such an early hour of the morning caught her attention. A disheveled man of quality exiting the inn from a side door caught her eye. He had obviously been drunk the night before, and she wrinkled her nose in distaste as he clasped a garishly painted woman to him and kissed her deeply. Sophia drew her head back into the coach. She felt sorry for women whose hopeless lives led them to such disreputable places, and she hated the men who bought their favors, thus encouraging such a life. It made no difference. Lord or peasant, all men used women for their own lust and in turn despised the women who serviced them.

The coach jerked through a big rut in the road, and Sophia's thoughts returned to what she might find when she arrived at Stonehurst. She wondered what Lord Alfred was like, but did not look forward to meeting the groom face to face.

CHAPTER 8

When Sophia's coach pulled into the courtyard of Stonehurst Manor, the entire household was in an uproar. After receiving word that her daughter had not been found, Elinor had collapsed and a doctor had been sent for. Lord Stonehurst was busy trying to organize the search party again. Wedding guests were leaving, having been told that the ceremony would not take place. It would make for good scandalous talk back home, but the guests couldn't wait and were talking in whispers among themselves. With the help of her footman, Sophia stepped unnoticed from the coach. Then, as she walked through the clusters of people, someone recognized her as Lord Stonehurst's eccentric sister and giggled. Sophia frowned and headed for the front door.

If the butler was surprised to see her, he did not show it, nor did he seem the least bit ruffled by the confusion around him. "Miss Stonehurst, welcome," he said calmly, as if he had been expecting her all along. "I will show you to the drawing room and fetch Lord Stonehurst."

She followed the stiffly formal servant to the drawing room and waited in its sunny warmth. She was impatiently pacing the room when her brother hurried in and took her in his arms. He was dressed for riding.

"How wonderful to see you, dear Sophia," he exclaimed as he kissed her cheeks. "I did not think you would be here for the wedding. I got your missive only days ago."

She kissed him back and noticed the dark circles under his eyes. "Clayton, it is good to see you too. I did not, however, come for the wedding. I had a feeling something was not right."

He threw up his hands in disgust. "Bah, there is no wedding anyway! Cassandra ran away last night and we have yet to find her."

"Ran away?" Sophia exclaimed. "But where could she have gone?"

"Where? Why, London, I'm sure. 'Tis the only other place she knows outside this county. Where else *could* she go?"

She didn't answer. Feeling certain that Cassandra was on her way to Dovecote, Sophia was relieved to hear that the searchers were on the wrong trail. "Where's Elinor?" she inquired.

"My wife is indisposed, as you can imagine, and totally useless. I am truly glad you are here, Sophia," he added tenderly. "You're the only female I know who can keep her head."

Sophia slipped off her gloves and untied her bonnet, which she placed carefully on a brocade-covered chair. She smoothed out her travel-worn muslin gown and sat on the couch without taking off her pelisse. She looked at her brother and raised her eyebrows. "Did Cassandra want to marry this man?"

"She said she didn't, but I thought she was just being difficult, as women are wont to do. Lord Alfred seemed a good match for her, and he was prepared to overlook some of her eccentricities."

"Eccentricities?"

"Oh," he answered evasively, "she was headstrong and willful."

Sophia looked into her brother's eyes and said, "I think there is more to all this than Cassandra's being headstrong and willful. I can't help you, Clayton, if you won't tell me the truth."

He paced the floor and rubbed his hands together, an old habit from their younger days when he tried to hide something from his sister. She always found him out, however. "Yes. Yes, you're right. There is more . . ."

Sophia waited for him to continue.

"I was too indulgent with her," he explained. "I always have been, you know." He paused, and Sophia smiled affectionately. "Then I permitted her to hang about the stables with a girl who insisted on dressing like a man. She gave Cassandra all sorts of foolish ideas." He was obviously uncomfortable with the subject and added quickly, "It was time for Cassandra to marry. Most women have children of their own by her age."

Sophia was silent for a moment, her index fingers templed at her lips in a gesture of deep thought. "You know," she said at last, "some women just aren't supposed to marry. Perhaps Cassandra is one of them."

"You speak nonsense," Clayton retorted. "All women need a husband to take care of them. You know I would have found one for you after father died, but you inherited that money and left."

Sophia silently thanked her luck — and her godmother who bequeathed the inheritance that permitted her to live the life she wanted. She wondered if Alex had found Cassandra, and if they were even now on their way to her small estate. She wanted to say something to her brother to ease his worry, but before she could speak again, the butler announced Lord Alfred. With a shock she recognized the man from outside the inn. He was now impeccably dressed, and she had to admit he had a nice turn to his leg. Then she noted his black eye and swollen jaw. So, he is a brawler too, she thought with contempt.

Lord Alfred bowed low to her. "Madame," he said before he turned to Lord Stonehurst's frowning countenance. "No news I presume."

"You dare show your face here?" Clayton replied with ill-concealed fury. "Your behavior last night was an insult. I would not have my Cassandra marry you now."

The younger man looked contrite, and Sophia guessed his drunkenness the night before hadn't been a new experience for him. She could only imagine what had transpired. She watched the emotions play across his face and wondered what he would say.

Lord Alfred cleared his throat. "I know I said some things last night that were uncalled for. I hope you will forgive me, sir. The attack on my person caused me to not think straight."

Sophia snorted. Her brother glanced at her in surprise. Lord Alfred knit his eyebrows together and curled his lip.

"Perhaps we should discuss this in private," the haughty young lord suggested.

"We have nothing to discuss that my sister cannot hear," Lord Stonehurst replied. "For that matter, there is nothing to discuss at all. As I said, the marriage is off."

Reddening, Lord Alfred nonchalantly picked an imaginary speck off his immaculate yellow jacket. "As you wish, but Cassandra is already the talk of the town. No man will have her now. Her reputation is ruined, but perhaps one day the idea of her inheritance will induce some poor fool to wed her."

In a voice sweet enough to melt sugar, Sophia asked, "Did you enjoy yourself at the tavern last night, my lord? I saw you leave this morning."

Lord Alfred glanced at her in surprise. "You must be mistaken, madam," he said, the haughty tone returning to his voice.

"Indeed, my lord," Sophia replied with a small bow of her head. She looked at him coolly, dismissing him with a flick of her eyelashes.

Lord Alfred turned on his heel and stalked out of the room. Sophia looked at her brother. She was disgusted. "If this is the man you wanted Cassandra to marry, it is no wonder she ran away. I would have done the same. You are lucky to be rid of him. I saw him with a tavern wench this morning. No telling what sort of diseases he might have."

Lord Stonehurst ignored her indelicate comment. "I must leave now and reorganize the searchers. I will send someone to fetch your bags and take them to the lavender guest room. It always was your favorite." He paused and took his sister's hands. "It is good that you are here. Elinor will need your support."

The Earl of Stonehurst then limped from the room, leaving his sister to wonder how soon she could get away without seeming ill-mannered. She had every confidence now that Cassandra was in Alex's good hands, and hoped they would get safely to Dovecote and wait.

By the end of November, Cassandra and Alex arrived at Dovecote. A buxom young maid, Kitty, told them where Cassandra's aunt had gone and that they were welcome and encouraged to stay. They accepted with delight, grateful to Aunt Sophia for her generosity, and at the same time enjoying the fact they would be alone for a few days.

"The first thing I want is a bath," Cassandra said as she headed up the stairs, stripping off the filthy black cloak and letting it fall to the ground. Her skin itched from the dust of their travels and from wearing the same clothes for almost two weeks. Kitty scurried to pick up the cloak and then rushed away to order the bath brought up.

"I must see to the horses first," Alex replied.

Cassandra stopped her ascent and turned. "You are not a servant here, Alex. Let someone else do that."

Alex smiled. "It is something I like to do. Besides, your aunt does not have much help. I want to do what I can."

"Very well," Cassandra answered, feeling a touch of her old grandeur return.

She continued up the stairs and entered what appeared to be a guest room. With a small cry of delight she recognized some of Alex's clothes. She scooped up a shirt and breathed in the smell of her. A while later, Kitty and another maid appeared with buckets of hot water for her bath. She quickly stripped off Alex's worn breeches and the torn and dirty gown, and instructed the maid to destroy them. Her undergarments could be cleaned and repaired. Then she settled gratefully into the steaming, rose-scented water. She luxuriated in the bath, soaping herself sensuously, letting the water trickle down between her breasts. It felt so good to be clean again. She lathered her hair and was squeezing water from the sponge onto her face when she heard someone enter the room.

"You are a fine sight to behold, milady."

Cassie's eyes flickered open. Alex stood before her, holding fresh buckets of hot water. The steam made Alex's chestnut hair curl around her face. Her shoulders looked so broad in the once-white linen shirt. Tucked into breeches, it accentuated her waist and slim hips. Scuffed black leather boots hugged her muscular calves. Cassandra could see the muscles in her forearms bulging slightly as she continued to hold the heavy buckets.

"You look like the first time I saw you," Cassandra said, smiling at the memory.

Alex laughed. "Well, you certainly don't look anything like the first time I saw you. And I must say, as beautiful as you look in crimson, I like you better this way."

Lowering her lashes, Lady Cassandra felt herself blush and reached for a towel. She couldn't believe she was behaving in such a brazen manner. Alex approached the tub.

"Would you like me to help you rinse your hair?"

Alex didn't wait for an answer, but began slowly, carefully to pour the water over the long tresses. When the soap was finally rinsed out, Cassandra squeezed the water out of her abundant hair. She stood and wrapped a thick towel around herself before she stepped out of the tub. She backed away from Alex, suddenly struck with shyness. Holding the towel tightly against her body, Cassandra sat on the bed and gazed at the woman who had caused such a turmoil in her life. She didn't know what her next course of action should be and wished her Aunt Sophia were home.

As if Alex sensed her mood, she said, "I will send Kitty up to help you dress. I am sure you are hungry too. When you are ready, come downstairs. I will be in the garden."

Cassandra was left alone in the room. She felt very foolish at her shyness with Alex. They had shared such intimacies that it was absurd for her to react so. Cassandra continued to clutch the towel to her, and Kitty soon appeared to help her dress. The maid unpacked the few items in her valise, which had somehow survived the journey. Cassandra chose an afternoon dress of lightweight wool. In the mirror, she saw that its deep plum color complemented her ash-blonde hair and blue eyes; the clinging fabric molded itself to her frame, accentuating her bosom more than would a low-cut bodice. Delicate edgings of white lace accented the high collar and called attention to her slim wrists. Her hair, still damp, she left loose to fall to her waist. Hoping Alex would be pleased with her appearance, she borrowed one of Aunt Sophia's straw bonnets and went to the garden.

The servants had set up a table outside in the sun. It was laden with good country fare — thick slices of home-baked bread, cold mutton and ham, chunks of cheese, wrinkled autumn apples, and scones with thick, rich, clotted cream. Although Cassandra would have preferred lemonade, the cook had prepared a pot of hot tea in consideration of the cool weather. The tea's enticing aroma held a hint of peppermint. She hadn't realized until then just how ravenous she was. The food she and Alex had shared on their journey had been very meager.

She glanced around for Alex before she sat at the table and waited. Soon realizing that no servant would appear, Cassandra helped herself to the delicious food. She put something of everything on her plate. She wasn't used to such simple fare. Most meals at Stonehurst Manor consisted of five to eight courses, each more rich and elaborate than the other. She couldn't remember when food had tasted so good. She was reaching for her third slice of bread when Alex came down the winding path. She carried a hoe and rake.

"Alex," Cassie exclaimed, "this food is excellent! Please, sit down and eat. I tried to wait, but I was so hungry. You must be starving too. What? Are you gardening?"

Alex stood before her. She bowed her head out of old habits. She still felt as if she was a servant. "I have already eaten. I am working in your aunt's rose garden. It has been neglected for a long time."

Cassandra gave an exasperated sigh. "Oh please, don't be so formal. You don't work for my father any longer. Sit and have some tea."

Alex sat, carefully placing the gardening tools against her chair. She knew the servants would not be scandalized because they were used to Aunt Sophia's eccentric ways. The two of them had often eaten together at this very table. When she awkwardly picked up one of the delicate porcelain tea cups, she noticed Cassandra hiding a smile behind her own cup. She felt so big and clumsy. I certainly wish I had one of the large earthenware mugs from Stonehurst, Alex thought, as she reached for the teapot.

They drank tea in companionable silence, happy just being together. Because the sun was not strong, Lady Cassandra took off her bonnet to let her hair flow free in the light breeze. Alex watched the slow rise and fall of Cassie's breast. She remembered when it quickened at her touch, and she began to feel tingly all over. When Cassie dipped her fingers into the clotted cream and then licked them off, Alex thought she would perish on the spot. It took all her self-control to sit there and behave like the lady her mother had taught her to be all those years ago. Finally, Alex could stand it no longer. She leapt to her feet and snatched up the gardening tools. Lady Cassandra looked at her in surprise.

"I must finish in the garden before it gets dark," Alex said as she hurried away, seemingly unaware that the sun would not set for hours yet.

Cassandra waited until Alex disappeared up the path before she burst into trills of laughter. She had been teasing Alex, and it pleased her that she could do so. She decided she would go to the rose garden too. Cassie walked sedately, her plum gown trailing over the wet green grass. Her clean hair blew gently behind her. The sun warmed her face and would bring out her freckles, but Aunt Sophia's bonnet lay forgotten on the grass.

Alex was already kneeling in the dirt, her sturdy fingers digging up weeds. Her back was to Cassandra, who stood and watched silently. She never tired of looking at Alex, especially when she was working. Weeding a garden was not as strenuous as mucking out a stable, she knew, but it nevertheless brought a sheen of sweat to Alex's skin. Cassandra gently touched her shoulder. Alex looked up in surprise, but smiled broadly when she saw who had disturbed her.

"I find it hot out here," she said casually as she

first fingered Alex's clean shirt and then let her fingers brush lightly across Alex's neck. "Don't you?"

"Not too hot."

Cassandra crossed her arms and tapped her foot. Her tall figure cast a shadow over Alex's frame. "Why don't you come up to your room and tell me about what you've been doing for my aunt?"

Hiding a smile, Alex replied, "I can tell you everything at dinner."

Sighing with mock impatience, Cassandra answered, "I really do think you should get out of the sun, Alex. You are much too brown already."

Alex capitulated easily. "Well yes, I do think it might be a trifle hot. Come, I will tell you what you want to know."

CHAPTER 9

Once in the room, Alex dropped all pretense and took hold of Cassandra. They folded their arms around each other, and Cassie lay her head on Alex's chest. Neither spoke, and Alex reveled in the feeling of holding and being held. She breathed in the scent of Cassie's freshly washed hair as she brushed her lips lightly across her lover's forehead.

"It is wonderful to hold you like this. I missed you terribly while I was here alone."

Cassandra nuzzled her breast. "I missed you too."

She shivered as she felt Cassie's hands travel

down her back, then cup her buttocks. She put her hands on Cassandra's shoulders and pushed her gently away so she could lean down and kiss her. The first kiss was electrifying; she felt the tingling all the way down to her toes. Cassandra moaned softly. Again the hands grazed her back, and Alex felt the power of her rippling muscles twitch beneath Cassie's nails. Alex kissed deeply, letting the tip of her tongue flick the roof of Cassandra's mouth. Her hands roamed over Cassie's sleek body; the tight woolen gown outlined every curve.

Then Cassie urged her backward toward the bed. They fell upon the soft eiderdown coverlet, clinging to each other and kissing passionately. Alex cursed her calloused fingertips as she fumbled with the lacings on the back of the plum-colored gown.

"How can you bear to wear this every day?" she asked.

Cassandra's eyes sparkled with laughter. "I usually have a lady's maid to dress me, remember? It's very easy once you get the knack, and I think it's time for you to get it, don't you?"

She growled and rolled Cassie onto her back. She pulled on the gown, which gave easily under her strong fingers. The resounding rip brought a gasp to Lady Cassandra's lips, but before she could protest, Alex kissed her again. She quickly drew the gown over Cassandra's hips, leaving her clad only in a thin chemise of soft silk over a corset of satin. More reluctant to tear the silken underclothes than the woolen gown, Alex carefully pulled the chemise off and untied the laces on the bodice of the corset. Her fingers shook with self-control. Her fumblings tangled the laces even more. She gulped in a deep breath as

Cassandra's breasts finally came free of the restricting material, the rosy nipples already hard. With a moan, Alex closed her lips over a puckered nipple and sucked it in. Cassandra answered with a tiny cry as she weaved her fingers into Alex's hair.

Cassie grabbed hold of her shoulders and tried to pull off her shirt. Alex chuckled. Cassie didn't have her strength. She made herself abandon Cassandra's breasts only long enough to undress. She was pleased when Cassandra roughly pulled off her own remaining underclothes. She kicked the coverlet from the bed, exposing cool scented sheets that felt wonderful and luxurious.

Time had no meaning as Alex kissed Cassie's face and throat, nibbling her way down over shoulders, breasts, and belly. Her fingers stroked satin-smooth thighs, dipping occasionally into wetness that flowed like honey under a hot sun. Cassandra responded with explorations of her own, as if eager to make Alex tremble as she herself trembled.

The late afternoon sun moved around the house, leaving the room in muted shadows. The lovers did not notice the darkening. Intent only on each other, Cassie and Alex delved into a new and exciting way of pleasure.

Alex's hands moved constantly over Cassandra's body. Then her mouth followed the same path. Her flicking tongue sent shivers up Cassandra's spine. Struggling to control her moans, she could not help but cry out when Alex's tongue unexpectedly flicked between her legs. Although blushing furiously at the intimacy of Alex's action, she found that she enjoyed the new sensation. It left her weak, unable to protest or to move Alex away. She arched her back, her fingers crushing the pillows that somehow wound up under her. Alex's broad shoulders spread her legs, and she bent her knees in response. Alex wrapped her arms under and around Cassandra's thighs and hips and rested her palms on Cassie's belly.

Time and space dissolved as Cassandra lost all sensation save that of Alex's mouth and gentle, probing tongue.

Alex breathed in the scent and taste of her. She didn't flinch when Cassie grabbed her shoulders or when fingernails drew her blood. She could only feel Cassie convulsing beneath her, taste the wetness that flowed into her mouth, and smell the woman-ripe scent of her. Even as Cassandra's body stilled its movement, she continued to lick and caress. She moved up, tasting the salty sweat that covered Cassandra's body like a fine mist. Her mouth covered Cassie's parted lips; their tongues met. Alex lay on top, their bodies pressed together tightly as they kissed. Then Cassandra pushed her away and tried to control her own heavy breathing. Alex's breathing was also quick.

"Do all lovers share such intimacy?" Cassandra gasped. Her glistening skin flushed a deeper red.

Alex grinned. "Not all. Only the lucky ones."

"Where did you learn such things?"

Alex rolled over onto her side and propped her head up on her hand so she could look at

Cassandra. "Do you always ask so many questions after someone has made love to you?" she asked sternly.
    Cassandra glanced at her sharply, relaxing when she saw Alex smiling broadly. She reached up to touch Alex's cheek. "Is it like this with men and women?"
    "I cannot speak for all women, but for me it would not be the same with a man. I find men repulsive. They are selfish creatures, like pigs rutting in a field."
    Cassie smothered a giggle. Alex frowned. Was Cassandra laughing at her? She didn't find men a laughing matter.
    "Oh pooh!" Cassandra said as she sat up and pushed Alex onto the pillows. "Don't look so cross. I am thinking of Lord Alfred, dressed in his best clothes, snuffling in a mud wallow. Now, let me see how good a pupil I am."
    Alex began to laugh, but Cassie crawled on top of her and began to kiss her all over. Using both instinct and imitation, she brought Alex to a gasping frenzy. Teasing, Cassie flicked her tongue over Alex's thighs, using her nails to trail a light path over her lover's body. Her long ash-blonde hair tickled, but it felt wonderfully soft and made Alex shiver and brought goose bumps to her skin. The sheets were no longer soft and cool, but damp and warm in a crumpled mass underneath them. Alex clenched and unclenched her hands, grabbing first the sheets and then handfuls of Cassandra's hair. She tried to be careful and not hurt her, but as Cassie's mouth descended onto her most private place, she grabbed

fistfuls of hair. Cassandra let out a sharp yelp, but as soon as Alex relaxed her hold, the soft tongue continued.

Cassandra savored the taste and smell of Alex. It was quite unlike anything she'd experienced before. Who would have thought a woman could teach her such things? Cassie made little moaning sounds in her throat, responding to the more audible groans coming from Alex. She felt Alex's legs tense and held onto muscular thighs as Alex arched her back and called out her name. Alex's hips bucked wildly, but Cassandra continued to lick and suck. She licked, more gently now, until Alex calmed and her panting lessened, then rose up to trail her hair over Alex's thighs and belly.

"Alex," Cassandra said softly and kissed her.

Their scents mingled as their lips met, each tasting and smelling herself on the other. Cassandra's hands rested on the pillow above Alex's head, while Alex embraced her. Alex's hair was a profusion of chestnut curls made almost black by its wetness; Cassandra's blonde tresses coiled like silken ribbons around both their bodies. They lay still for a moment, then Cassandra rolled off Alex and rested beside her.

As she listened to the beating of her own heart, Cassandra noted with surprise that darkness had descended outside. In the dim light of the room, she made out the pale shape of Alex lying beside her. The twin mounds of Alex's breasts glowed with a sweaty sheen. Cassandra rested her hand on Alex's moist thigh. Alex placed her own hand on top of Cassandra's.

Alex broke the silence. "I love you, Cassie. You are more than I ever desired. What have I done to deserve you?"

"You are kind ... and gentle ... and strong ... and beautiful," Cassandra answered, rising to punctuate her words with kisses. "You're everything a woman could want."

"I can't give you the protection of my name, or a big estate. I am but a poor farmer's daughter, but you ... you are a lady, an earl's daughter. I couldn't bear it if you lost the respect you deserve."

Cassandra felt a twinge of fear at Alex's words. She had never fully considered all that she might lose. She knew that society looked askance at unmarried women. She thought of her Aunt Sophia, who, despite her independent though modest wealth, was still whispered about in the drawing rooms of Lord Stonehurst's friends and acquaintances. Cassandra took her hand from Alex's leg and shivered.

"What's wrong, Cassie," Alex exclaimed, "did I frighten you?" She sat up and squinted, peering at Cassandra's face in the darkness.

"No, Alex," she lied, "you didn't frighten me. Don't worry about me. I never liked the idea of marriage."

"I will take care of you, Cassie, whatever I have to do. I will make you happy. I promise."

Cassandra reached up for her. She smoothed the chestnut hair with her hands and kissed Alex's cheeks. "Yes, I know you will," she said. "We shall take care of each other. Now, let us get up."

Alex leapt out of bed and lit a candle. Cassandra lay in the flickering light and smiled when Alex looked at her, feeling at once beautiful and vulnerable under Alex's gaze. As Alex lit more candles in the room, the romantic light flattered Alex's wonderful body, highlighting her long, shapely legs and broad shoulders. Her breasts swayed gently with every movement. Cassandra watched with unabashed pleasure, thinking all the while that Alex was the most beautiful sight she had ever seen.

She jumped out of bed before she could be tempted to drag Alex back into it. The servants must already be wondering where they were. Surely it must be way past the dinner hour! After giving herself a quick sponge bath from the porcelain basin and pitcher, Cassandra dressed in a dove-white silk dinner gown. It took her some time to comb the tangles out of her hair and she wished briefly for a maid, even if it was Lizzie. Before she finished, Alex had long been washed and dressed.

"Did any of that work in the stable teach you to handle a comb?" Cassandra asked with an impatient yank on a particularly stubborn knot.

"Well," Alex answered with a grin, "I did use a curry comb on the horses. Somehow though, I don't think horse hair is quite the same as yours, except perhaps its tail."

Cassie threw the silver-plated comb at her in mock ire. "The day my hair resembles a horse's tail is the day I cut it off."

"Come, my lady," Alex said as she proffered her

arm. "Let us go to dinner. I am sure Cook is wondering where we are. It is a trifle late, don't you think?"

Once downstairs, the lovers found the table in the modest dining room indeed set for their evening repast. It turned out they weren't quite as late as they thought. Cassandra was surprised to find a place set for Alex, although she had been prepared to order it done. She didn't realize just how keen Aunt Sophia's loyal servants were. Apparently, they had quickly discerned that Alex was more to the Lady Cassandra than just a casual servant. Besides, their absent mistress had asked Alex to dine with her on several occasions. Because of Alex's fine manners and speech, they must have innocently assumed her to be a gently bred lady whose eccentricities included wearing men's clothing and working in gardens and stables.

The repast was not quite as plain as the one Cassandra had enjoyed earlier in the garden. It was still simple by aristocratic standards, consisting of only three courses instead of the usual five to eight. Once their dessert of dried fruit and sherbet was finished, Alex and Cassandra enjoyed a cup of coffee.

"This tastes wonderful," Cassandra said as she sipped her second cup. "Where did Aunt Sophia learn about this coffee?"

"From her American friend. Jennifer I think her name is. She's a writer or something of that sort from Boston. Maybe a journalist."

"A female journalist?" Cassandra exclaimed, "How

exciting! Papa would never even let me read the newspaper. He says it isn't something a well-bred young lady should concern herself with, for it has all manner of unsuitable stories in it. I think he protected me too much."

"I can understand why he would want to protect you. He loves you, as I do."

Cassandra tossed her head impatiently. "Loving someone doesn't mean you have to keep them in ignorance. I should have visited Aunt Sophia more often. Then I would have met her journalist friend and learned to drink coffee much sooner. How did she meet Jennifer?"

"Aunt Sophia mentioned meeting her in London. I think the war has prevented her from returning to America. I wouldn't want to be in her shoes, living among the enemy."

"War is men's business. And they don't think of women as dangerous. I'm sure Aunt Sophia would have invited her to stay here if she was in any peril."

Alex didn't answer but gazed silently at the woman she loved. Her mind went back to the first day she and Lady Cassandra came face to face, and she smiled as she remembered the shocked look on Cassie's face. Things certainly had changed since then, she thought. They had just shared a meal as equals after an afternoon of lovemaking that went beyond her wildest fantasy. Alex wanted this day and night to last forever. She was brought out of her reverie by fingers tapping on her arm.

"What are you thinking, Alex?" Cassandra asked with some concern. "You look so serious."

Alex ran her fingers through her unruly hair. "I was only thinking of the day I met you." She looked down at Cassandra's fingers resting on her arm. "Come, let us go into the parlor and you can play something for me on the pianoforte. I've never heard you play, but I can tell from your hands that you are excellent."

Cassandra blushed and smiled as she stood and held out her hand. Alex stood and guided Cassandra's hand into the crook of her arm. They walked sedately out of the dining room, Alex shortening her normally long stride to accommodate Cassandra's more demure walk. They were almost matched in height, but their bodies were very different. Alex's broad shoulders tapered down to a slim waist and softly rounded hips. The tight men's breeches she always wore showed off shapely thighs and calves that any man of fashion would envy. Cassie was also slim, but her curves were only hinted at, covered as they were by the fashionable silk gown. The lightweight corset she wore pushed her breasts up and together, but the bit of perfumed lace tucked into her cleavage preserved her modesty.

In the parlor, a fire burned low. Cassandra lit a few candles near the pianoforte, just enough so she could read the music notes off the pages that Alex turned for her. She had a beautifully trained voice. The music soared through the room, sending shivers down Alex's spine. Much later, seeing that Cassandra was tired, Alex closed the book and smiled at her.

"I knew you would play well because you have

such beautiful hands," she murmured as she brought Cassie's fingers to her lips.

Cassandra rose from the bench and slid her hands around Alex's neck. They started to kiss. Suddenly, the candles sputtered out, plunging them into darkness. Laughing, they fled the room.

CHAPTER 10

Sophia counted the days until she could leave Stonehurst Manor without appearing rude. She spent the hours trying to calm her frantic sister-in-law, who worried about the fate that had befallen her daughter. Lord Stonehurst sent out search parties daily, to no avail. Sophia was beginning to worry herself. She was sure she would have received word from her niece or Alex once they reached Dovecote. When no message came, she dispatched a letter herself. It would be days before she heard anything, and meanwhile she had to help calm Clayton and Elinor's fears.

"I am sure she is safe," Sophia said one mild December afternoon on the terrace as she poured tea. She wished she had coffee instead. "We would have heard if she'd been found on the road somewhere."

Elinor uttered a small cry of despair and wrung her hands repeatedly. Sophia wanted to snatch at them to stop her. She was not a heartless woman, but Lady Stonehurst's self-serving dramatics were becoming intolerable. Sophia couldn't count the times she'd had to burn feathers or find smelling salts to revive her constantly swooning sister-in-law. She had always resented women who made it a practice to exhibit socially acceptable feminine weaknesses in order to be the center of attention themselves.

"What if she's been delivered to a brothel?" Lady Stonehurst wailed.

"My dear! Remember yourself!" the earl remonstrated, shocked that his wife would talk of such things.

"I couldn't bear it. Oh, the humiliation. First the scandal of the wedding, and now, my Cassandra, a fallen woman. Who will marry her now?"

Sophia snorted in disgust. "Is that all you care about? I wouldn't blame Cassandra if she never married. I should think you'd be more concerned about her safety than who you'll marry her off to."

"All this shows is that she needs a good man to control her," Lady Stonehurst insisted. "Clayton and

I were too lenient with her because she is our only child. Oh, I should have married her to Lord Alfred when he first asked for her hand after the ball."

Sophia set her tea cup rattling onto its saucer. "That man is despicable. How can you even think of marrying her to him? Leave her alone. When she is found, she can live with me."

Lady Stonehurst looked at her askance. Sophia knew Elinor only tolerated her because she was Clayton's sister. Elinor probably believes Cassandra's reputation will be ruined beyond repair if she lives with me, she mused. She was sure Elinor had heard the whispers about her peculiar ways, perhaps even the allegations that she preferred members of her own sex. So be it, Sophia thought. Her way of life was no doubt beyond Elinor's comprehension. Indeed, if Sophia guessed properly, she had already forgotten Alex's existence.

"Thank you, Sophia," Elinor acknowledged politely, "but when Cassandra is found we will take care of her in the proper fashion. We might send her to a convent until all this scandal blows over."

Clayton responded to his wife's comments by rolling his eyes and shaking his head. Sophia curled her lip and didn't answer. Really! How could her brother have married such a ninny? A convent, of all things! Why, they weren't even Catholic. She stood up abruptly. "If you will excuse me. I have a slight headache and will rest before dinner."

Sophia sat at the desk in her room writing a letter to her American friend now residing in London, Jennifer Adams. England was at war with America, so Jennifer had decided not to return home, which made Sophia very happy. A knock announced a maid with a letter. Recognizing Lady Cassandra's handwriting, she hastily tore the letter open and read eagerly. At last, her niece had written in response to her urgent message. All was well; Cassandra and Alex had arrived safely at Dovecote two weeks earlier and they looked forward to her return. Jubilant, Sophia determined to leave at first light. She could be home in time for the holidays. She summoned a maid to begin packing her belongings. The question now remained on how to explain the situation to her brother and sister-in-law without their immediately demanding Lady Cassandra's return.

After much thought, Sophia decided to be candid with her brother. She didn't think he would be as unreasonable as his wife seemed inclined to be. She knew he harbored no great liking for Lord Alfred and genuinely wanted his daughter to be happy. She tracked him down in his library. His gruff voice bade her to enter.

Lord Stonehurst sat behind his great desk, going over his neglected account books. Sophia was shocked at how old he looked. The strain of the past weeks had taken its toll. She walked over and stood in front of the desk, looking down at him.

"Dear brother," she said gently, "you look so very tired. I am afraid I haven't been much help, have I?"

Clayton raised his worn eyes to hers. "It hasn't been easy for you either, Sophia. My wife has never approved of you, but you know that. I am grateful for your support. Don't ever doubt that."

She leaned over the desk and gently placed her hand over his. It was a small gesture of comfort to a brother whom she had worshiped as a child. She thought it a shame that they had grown apart as adults.

He gave her a grateful smile. "I truly am glad to have you back with me. I am so afraid for my daughter, and I know you understand."

Sophia sat in the comfortable chair before his desk. Feeling a bit nervous, she automatically wished for a fan to give her hands something to do. "What is it you are afraid of?"

"I don't want to lose her like I lost you." He sighed. "Society puts ridiculous pressures on us. Sometimes we do things to the people we love because of stupid conventions that, underneath it all, we really don't believe in."

Sophia realized what Clayton was trying to tell her. She still remembered the cruel things people said about her because of the way she chose to live. It had hurt that her beloved brother hadn't supported her, but she had forgiven him long ago.

"I don't blame you for anything, Clayton. Now, let us forget the past. I know where Cassandra is."

The earl leapt to his feet. "What?"

"I received a letter from her just this afternoon, and I will tell you presently ... Provided you give me your word that you will not interfere with her in any way."

"Interfere? Cassandra is under age. She still requires my protection."

"Just promise that you will trust me. You know I wouldn't let anything happen to her."

Lord Stonehurst shook his head and sat down

again. What his sister was asking went against all propriety. What would people say? Then he remembered how the wedding guests reacted to the news that there would be no wedding. They were careful not to speak so he could hear, but he saw the sly smiles and derisive looks, the whispered condemnation. What did he care any more for conventions? He wouldn't want to see those hypocrites again. If anyone could protect his Cassandra, it would be his sister.

"You have my word, Sophia."

Sophia breathed a sigh of relief and rose from her chair. "She has made it to my estate and awaits me there."

He put his head in his hands, hiding the grateful tears that came unbidden to his eyes with the news that his beloved daughter was well and safe. Sophia stood silently, letting him weep. Once again in control of his emotions, he rose and came around the desk until he stood next to her. He brusquely dashed the last tear from his eye.

He took her hands. "My wife will not approve, but I leave Cassandra in your capable hands. I think maybe you understand her more than we do."

Sophia hugged him. "Thank you. I will be leaving first thing in the morning. So that you may talk to Elinor in private, I will take a tray in my room tonight."

Sophia stood on tiptoe and patted his cheek in a gesture of sisterly affection before leaving. When she reached the door, he called to her. "Is Alex with her?"

Her hand on the doorknob, she answered without turning around. "Yes. Alex is with her."

The library door closed gently behind her. Lord Stonehurst returned to his chair and lay his head in his arms on the desk. He would not interfere in his daughter's life again, but he was saddened by the sudden realization that his family name would die with him and that the bulk of his fortune would go to an unknown distant male cousin. In his will, he would make provisions for his only child, but being an unmarried female, she could never inherit the full family fortune, which would have gone to her husband anyhow. How would he tell Elinor she would never be a grandmother?

At dawn, Sophia boarded her well-traveled coach for the long journey north. She left without saying goodbye, knowing her sister-in-law would not want to see her. Going to the library to return some books the night before, she had heard Elinor crying.

Sophia felt a pang of grief when she thought of leaving her poor brother, but she was glad to be going home now. She truly missed Dovecote when she was away, which was the major reason why she didn't travel much. The early December air had a distinct chill. Sophia knew it would snow in Northumberland sooner than it would in Cambridgeshire. Even now the first snowfall might be covering Dovecote.

Pushing her coachman and horses as much as possible without abusing them, she was ecstatic to see her modest manor as, days later, the carriage crested the last hill on the road home. Even the horses seemed to know they were near familiar territory and quickened their pace. The coachman flicked his whip at the horses to make them go faster. They didn't need much urging as they thundered toward clean hay and fresh water and delicious oats.

As they entered the courtyard, Cassandra ran out to greet her aunt. She certainly doesn't look the part of a lady of high fashion, Sophia thought as she noted the plain mouse-brown dress of worsted wool and the loosely flowing locks of ash-blonde hair bound only with a scarlet band. Cassandra flung her arms around her aunt's neck, and Sophia noted a faint odor of beeswax and lemon and wondered if her niece was becoming domestic. Such a smell was usually associated with the maids who polished furniture.

"Let me look at you," Sophia exclaimed as she clasped Cassandra's hands. "Why, I would never know you to be the Lady Cassandra if it wasn't for your glorious hair. What has become of my very proper niece?"

"Oh, Aunt Sophia, I have been so happy. I've even learned to work in the greenhouse." She raised her hands. "Look!" she exclaimed proudly. "Dirty fingernails!"

Sophia examined the delicate hands in front of her. Cassie did indeed have dirt under her nails, but they were still long and perfectly shaped. Sophia put her arm around Cassandra's waist and walked with her into the house. Her stern butler barely smiled as he ushered them in, but Kitty let loose a squeal of pure delight when she saw her mistress. Sophia allowed Kitty to squeeze her in a tight hug. She knew most people would be appalled at such familiar behavior from a servant. At one time even Cassandra surely would have been, but now she just stood back and smiled. Laughing, Sophia instructed Kitty to unpack the trunk that was being hauled up the front steps, and then turned to her niece again.

"I am dying for a cup of coffee. Come, let us go into the parlor. I want to know everything that has happened since you disappeared from your father's house."

She stripped off her bonnet and pelisse and dropped them onto a chair. The butler discreetly picked them up to deliver to the laundry, where the travel dust would be brushed and washed away. The two women went into the sunny parlor. A tray laden with a coffee pot and a plate of delicate pastries already awaited them. Asking Cassandra to pour, Sophia struggled to take off her boots. She let out a sigh of relief when she succeeded.

"It is so good to be home," she said. "To be truthful, I find your mother's company very tedious."

Cassandra laughed, and then became sober. "How are my parents? Are they very cross with me?"

"No, your father understands. I think he realizes now what kind of man Lord Alfred really is." Cassandra wrinkled her nose at the mention of her intended bridegroom. "Anyway," she continued, "your father has granted permission for you to stay with me. I don't think he will trouble you. He loves you very much and maybe when things have settled down more he will visit."

Cassandra sipped her coffee. "And Mama?"

"She is another matter, but give her time. She would still marry you off if she could. If not to Lord Alfred, then to someone else."

"I will never marry," Cassandra said defiantly.

"Where is Alex?" Sophia asked, remembering the cause of Cassandra's flight.

"Out riding," Cassandra answered. "She's breaking in a new horse. One of your neighbors asked if we had someone who could do it until they hire their own. She's new I think, the neighbor, I mean."

A new neighbor, Sophia mused, and a woman. She hoped to meet this neighbor for herself soon. In the meantime, she wanted to know every detail of Cassandra's daring escape and the adventures that had befallen her and Alex.

Nearly two hours later, Cassandra had exhausted her account of all that had happened. Although she found the details of Cassandra's escape very exciting, Sophia was particularly interested in hearing about the improvements that Alex had made in running the estate. No one had really shown an interest in it before, least of all herself. As long as the land was self-sufficient she was happy. She was most heartened to hear of the interest of others to pay for Appleton's stud services for their mares. It was gratifying to know her brother's best horseflesh was now residing at Dovecote.

It was then that Sophia realized just how much her niece had changed. This young noblewoman, whose only concern months ago was the quality of the material in a new gown, was discussing matters not thought to be proper topics for a lady of quality. In fact, some of these topics were considered downright scandalous. If her sister-in-law could hear Cassandra talking about breeding mares, she would swoon for days.

A noise caused them both to turn. Silhouetted in

the doorway was Alex, freshly bathed after her hard ride. Her damp hair curled around her face. Her skin glowed with a clean healthy look, and the golden-brown eyes were bright with welcome. As Alex walked in, grinning broadly, Sophia marveled anew at her sinewy strength and good looks. It was nice to know some things never changed, she thought, as she rose to embrace the woman who had come to mean so much to her only niece, and to herself.

CHAPTER 11

The winter months deepened. Early 1814 passed joyously for Aunt Sophia and her young houseguests. Aunt Sophia received money from her brother for Cassandra's care, which she promptly turned over to her niece. It was time for Cassandra to learn how to manage her own financial affairs, her aunt had told her, and to this end Sophia had begun to teach her accounting. Alex still performed chores in the stable, but she spent more time inside now. Many an afternoon found Alex reading a book while her lover embroidered or played the pianoforte.

Cassandra wrote often to her father, wanting him to know she was happy. She occasionally received a letter from her mother, who mentioned a different eligible bachelor's name every time. She only wrote once about Lord Alfred. It seemed there was some scandal with the vicar's daughter so he had fled the country for a bit. Cassandra's mother was sure the tales weren't true. She still thought her headstrong daughter would come to her senses.

Sometimes, while Aunt Sophia and Cassie had their accounting lesson, Alex would fill out records of the changes she had made to make Dovecote lands more profitable. She had already established new tenant farmers who would plant more crops come spring, and Appleton's reputation as a superb stud stallion was spreading. She dreamed of owning and maintaining a horse farm that people would come from all over the country to see. She accepted Aunt Sophia's higher-than-normal wages, and carefully put the money away for the day when she could buy her own acreage.

When Jennifer managed to travel up from London, the four women passed pleasant afternoons playing cards. Sophia and Cassandra taught Alex and Jennifer the games whist, loo, and faro. Sometimes, Jennifer would regale them with tales of America, making them laugh with her comparisons of Bostonians and Londoners. That England was at war with America was a subject politely avoided.

One early March morning, Alex woke before the sun lit the sky. The room was in complete darkness.

Heavy brocade drapes on the windows kept out not only any bit of light, but also the damp cold. As her eyes adjusted to the gloom, Alex glanced around at the now familiar surroundings. Beside her, Cassie slept deeply. Alex grinned as she remembered their torrid lovemaking from the night before. The bedclothes were still a jumbled mass winding seductively through and around their legs beneath the heavy coverlet. Cassandra's smooth thigh peeked out, and Alex placed her calloused hand upon it. Cassandra stirred at the touch but did not waken. It would be so easy to stay in bed, Alex thought as she sat up and threw her long legs over the side. She shivered at the winter chill in the air. The fire had long since burnt out.

Treading quietly, Alex went to the hearth and lit a fire. Then she splashed freezing water from the porcelain basin onto her face, washing the last traces of sleep from her eyes. She dressed in front of the quickly blazing fire. She wore warm woolens beneath her normal men's attire, the linen shirts long ago traded for woolen ones. Her clothes were cold as she put them on, but it was something she was used to from long years of living as a servant. They did not usually have the luxury of fireplaces in their dreary attic rooms or lofts above the stable.

Once dressed, Alex walked over to the bed and stood looking down at Cassandra. It was still a wondrous thing to her that they lived openly in love. She cared naught for the luxuries she now enjoyed except that they gave Cassie joy. Alex would be happy enough in a tenant farmer's mud-and-straw cottage if Cassie lived there with her. She reached down to brush a long strand of golden hair from her face, then leaned over and kissed her gently before turning to leave the room. She opened the drapes just a bit so Cassie wouldn't awaken in total darkness.

Closing the door quietly behind her, Alex swiftly descended the stairs and entered the kitchen. Servants were already busy preparing breakfast. They smiled a welcome but did not stop their tasks. Alex breathed in the scent of baking bread. It wouldn't be ready for some time, yet she needed to fortify herself for the early chores in the stable. Helping herself to boiling water, she prepared a large mug of tea, liberally spooning in honey, and then slathered a chunk of day-old bread with more of it. If she had time, she would return later to eat a formal breakfast in the dining room.

When she finished eating, Alex made a side trip to the greenhouse to cut a dozen yellow roses. She was glad that Aunt Sophia's gardener had mastered the complicated feat of growing the temperamental blooms in the dead of winter. And yellow ones just happened to be Cassie's favorite. Locating a crystal vase on the pianoforte in the parlor, she returned to the kitchen. Filling the vase with water, she then arranged the flowers as best she could. She called to a young maid who was preparing to polish Aunt Sophia's silver. The girl scurried over, eager to please Alex, whom she regarded with awe.

"Yes, ma'm," the girl said, dropping to a quick curtsy.

Alex frowned slightly. She didn't want the servants bowing to her, but she knew the girl wouldn't listen and changed her frown into a smile.

"Could you please take these to Lady Cassandra's room? Be very careful. They are heavy."

The young maid took the vase. Alex followed her out of the kitchen and watched her walking carefully up the stairs. She wished she could take them up herself, but she knew if she did she would climb back into bed with Cassie. With a sigh, Alex left the house and walked briskly to the stable, last week's snow crunching beneath her boots. The morning was very cold, the sky gray. It felt like it could snow again.

Cassandra stretched like a cat in the big bed she shared with Alex, flexing her fingers and toes. It was still hard for her to believe the changes in her life. It seemed like only yesterday that she was preparing for her debut ball — that the most important thing in her life was a new gown of raspberry silk. Oh, there was no denying that at times she missed that life. Being pampered did have its advantages. Not that she suddenly had to fend totally for herself now, but she tried to be more self-sufficient. Although finally sleeping in the guest bedroom of a manor house, Cassie knew that Alex still considered herself a servant. It made Alex uncomfortable when people she thought of as her equals waited on her hand and foot, but she still expected them to show Lady Cassandra the deference due her.

Discovering the empty pillow, Cassandra realized she'd slept longer than intended. Alex was already up, working. The pale sunlight peeking through the crack in the drapes told her it was still early morning. At least it wasn't almost midday, which was the time she used to get up when she lived at Stonehurst Manor. Her body still tingled from the passionate lovemaking of the previous night. She ran her fingers down her stomach and played with the curls nestled between her legs. Sighing, she relinquished her self-exploration and sat up. Sometimes she wished Alex would remain abed, just so they could make love.

The vase full of hothouse flowers caught her eye and she smiled with pleasure. The only ones to be had at this time of year came from Aunt Sophia's greenhouse. Alex had asked the gardener to cultivate Lady Cassandra's favorite pale yellow roses so she could have them year-round. Cassie leapt out of bed and buried her nose into the blooms, breathing in their delicate sweet smell. It was so nice when Alex surprised her this way.

She pulled open the drapes. The sun made her blink. Turning, she noticed the fire burning low and added more logs. As she washed, she remembered that Aunt Sophia had mentioned something last night about a dinner party. The thought made her happy. As much as she loved her new life, she couldn't help but miss the fun she had at Stonehurst with all the balls and dinner parties. It had been months since she'd danced. If the truth were known, there were times, though few, when she was very bored. Alex, she felt, still spent too much time working.

Cassandra tugged the bell cord and soon Kitty

arrived to help her to dress. The maid chose a long-sleeved heavy cotton morning gown of deep lavender. Unlike the elaborate gowns Lady Cassandra wore at Stonehurst Manor, this dress was simple in style and much more suitable for the cold weather. Thinking of the fashionable but impractical thin muslin gowns she used to wear even in the dead of winter sent shivers down Cassandra's spine.

Cassie decided to let Kitty comb and style her long hair, instead of simply gathering it into a loose chignon herself. Using a hot iron, Kitty first painstakingly curled Lady Cassandra's thick tresses, then laced a matching lavender ribbon through. Kitty didn't seem to mind acting as Cassandra's personal maid. If it gives Kitty pleasure, Cassandra had told Alex one day, it gives me pleasure.

Cassandra turned her head back and forth to see herself in the mirror. "It looks beautiful, Kitty. Thank you. Is my aunt up yet?"

"Yes, ma'am," Kitty replied with a self-satisfied smile. "She's with Cook, plannin' the dinner menu fer tonight. That American girl's due to be arrivin', she is."

Cassandra slid her feet into leather slippers. With one last glance in the mirror, she followed Kitty out of the bedroom and descended the long staircase. The enticing aroma of breakfast led her into the dining room. She hoped Alex hadn't eaten yet, but was disappointed to find her place cleared already. After helping herself at the sideboard, Cassandra poured a cup of strong coffee and settled down to wait for Aunt Sophia.

"Ah, you're up," Aunt Sophia noted as she glided

into the room, the hem of her forest-green gown whispering across the cold wooden floor. "I've already eaten, but I will share a cup of coffee with you."

"How are the plans for dinner coming?" Cassandra asked between mouthfuls of eggs and kidneys. "Is it going to be a large party?" She couldn't keep the anticipation out of her voice. Jennifer so far had been their only visitor.

Aunt Sophia smiled. "Not too large — there will be six." She took a sip of coffee. "Jennifer is coming," she continued, "and of course there will be you and Alex. I know Alex doesn't like formal affairs, but I expect you to convince her to participate. I'm sure we can find something suitable for her to wear. I've invited our new neighbors. They are quite nice, so I've heard."

"The married couple?" Cassandra held her breath.

"Actually no. It's the two women, recently come from London. Both quite wealthy from what I understand. I have been sadly remiss in not meeting them these many months."

Cassandra smiled and munched on her bread. She had hoped it would be the two women. She hunched over her plate, elbows on the table.

Aunt Sophia frowned. "Don't sit like a peasant, Cassandra!"

Blushing furiously, she dropped her elbows off the table and placed her hands demurely in her lap. "Yes, Aunt Sophia," she responded quietly.

"Perhaps it would be better for you to return to your parents for a bit."

Cassandra stared at her aunt in surprise. "Oh no! You can't mean it. I don't ever want to go back there."

Her eyes twinkling, Aunt Sophia took a last drink of her coffee and rose from the table. "Well, don't let me catch you acting like a peasant girl again. I know I am not strict like your father, but you are still a lady. I don't want him to regret allowing you to stay. Now, don't look so glum. Go and see what your Alex is up to."

Relieved that Aunt Sophia was only teasing, Cassandra rose also and followed her out of the dining room, just as the servants came into the room and began to clear away the breakfast dishes. She knew that Alex had taken her own dishes to the kitchen.

"How long will Jennifer be staying this time?" she asked.

Aunt Sophia smiled. "For three weeks, but I hope it will be longer."

Cassie hoped too that Jennifer would stay. She knew her aunt was very fond of her, and the four of them got along so famously. She decided to check the stables first. It was Alex's favorite place.

In the stables, Alex was heating up the metal rod she would need to shoe three newly purchased horses. She was very grateful she'd learned the blacksmith trade from Harry. She certainly did miss him though, because there was always more to learn. There had been many a time she had burned her hands because of clumsy technique. Still, she saved Aunt Sophia money by being able to do most things herself.

Given the freezing winter air outside, Alex

enjoyed the intense heat of the forge. She was always careful, but still felt sometimes as if her face were scorching. The sweat dripped off her brow as she leaned into the flames to check the already glowing metal. As per Harry's instructions, she wore a heavy leather apron for protection against flying sparks. When she had assured herself that everything was satisfactory, Alex stood and stretched. She sensed another presence and turned to find Cassandra hovering near the door. A welcoming smile cracked the fine powdering of soot that covered her skin.

"You look like a street urchin," Lady Cassandra laughed.

Alex selfconsciously wiped her hand across her face, trying to clean off a bit. Instead, she felt the soot and grime smear. Lady Cassandra burst into uncontrollable laughter. Alex stared at her, then joined in the laughter. She made a threatening move, as if to rub her sooty hands all over Cassandra's lavender gown.

Cassandra backed against the wall as Alex approached. She felt her heart begin to beat faster. Her breath came in shallow gasps. When Alex stood in front of her and leaned forward so her hands rested on the wall on both sides of Cassie's head, she sucked in her breath and felt herself grow wet between her legs. She gazed into Alex's golden-brown eyes and read the passion lurking there.

This is ludicrous, she thought, as she put her hands on Alex's head to pull her down for a kiss.

She tasted charcoal but it didn't matter. Alex groaned and pulled Cassie into a strong embrace. Despite the sweat and grime and her own fine cotton dress, she didn't pull away as Alex's hands entwined themselves into her hair. So what if she left streaks of black ashes? Cassie didn't care.

"Cassie," Alex moaned, "we have to stop this."

"No," she murmured. "No one will come in. You know the others find it too hot in here."

Cassandra had her hands around Alex's back and began to fumble with the knotted lacings on the apron. Alex stopped her.

"You are crazy, my love." Alex held Cassandra's hands tightly in her own. "Someone is bound to find us. And look at you! How will you explain the soot on your person?"

Cassandra tried to withdraw her hands, but Alex held fast. "You forget, we are no longer at my papa's house. I don't have to explain myself to anyone."

"I can't say no to you, Cassie!" Alex exclaimed, and swept her into her strong arms.

Cassandra put her arms around Alex's sinewy shoulders and let herself be carried into an adjacent empty stall that had been newly cleaned and spread with fresh hay. The excitement brought a flush to her cheeks; her heart thudded against her ribs. As Alex tried to lower both of them into the hay, Cassie kissed her deeply. The strong woman stumbled, and they fell laughing, arms and legs flailing. The hay was soft, yet prickled Cassandra's neck. Her carefully coiffed hair had come undone and was falling down around her shoulders, but she didn't care. They lay back, arms out flung, still laughing. She sat up suddenly and leaned over Alex.

Her kiss was full of wanting; her tongue probed the inside of Alex's mouth. She started to unbutton Alex's shirt, but the heavy material made it difficult. Alex decided to help her and as their fingers touched, Cassie felt a surge of emotion that made her undress more feverishly.

The crackling flames from the forge flickered, breaking the silence and creating dancing shadows along the wall. Alex lay next to Cassie. They were both naked and breathing deeply. Their lovemaking, intense and brief, had left them both exhausted. Alex was aware that at any moment someone could come in and catch them, but she liked the danger. Their flushed skin glistened with sweat, the droplets shimmering like a diamond veil in the red-gold firelight. At last, Cassandra sat up. Her blonde hair was a knotted, straw-covered mass of confusion framing her soot-smudged face.

Alex looked at her and laughed. She couldn't stop laughing.

One look at Alex and Cassie started laughing too. "You really are a sight!" She leaned over and kissed her lover. "We must get dressed," she said breathlessly.

Alex stood and scrambled into her clothes. She left the stall and then returned carrying a bucket filled with freezing water and lifted it easily. "It's not much, but you could at least wash your face," she said with a hint of laughter as she placed the bucket near the bed of hay. The water sloshed over and sprinkled Cassie's feet. The icy droplets made her shriek.

"You can't expect me to wash my face with that!" she cried indignantly as she gathered her clothing.

"In the attic bedrooms of manor houses, the servants do it every day," Alex replied matter-of-factly. And, she thought, they lay the fires in the more luxurious bedrooms well before dawn. What was a little cold?

Lady Cassandra's fire-flushed face darkened to a deeper red. Alex detected guilt in her harsh words. "Don't blame me for the troubles in the world. I did not make the rules. I didn't choose to be born a Stonehurst!"

Her words stung. "Cassie, I was not trying to judge . . ." she began, but she was already gone.

CHAPTER 12

Unheedful of her disheveled, dirty appearance, Cassandra rushed to the house, cursing as she skidded over slick snow. She wondered how she could possibly sneak into the house undetected, but when she burst through the front doors, no servants lingered in the foyer. She flew up the stairs, leaving a weaving trail of wet soot. Once in the bedroom she shared with Alex, Cassandra tugged impatiently on the bell cord to summon Kitty. Feeling as if Alex had scolded her, anger and shame burned her face and diminished their morning lovemaking. She stripped off her ruined gown and threw it on the floor. Shivering in silk underclothes, she tugged on the bell cord again.

"Where is that woman?" she asked aloud, aggrieved. A rapping on the door was her answer.

Retreating into the shadows of the canopied bed, she called for Kitty to enter. If the maid thought it strange that her mistress cowered behind the bed drapes, she gave no indication.

"Yes, milady?"

"I want hot water for a bath immediately. And something hot to drink. Coffee, I think, with lots of cream."

"Yes, milady." Kitty turned to go.

Still feeling guilty over the misunderstanding with Alex in the stable, Cassandra impulsively called out. "Kitty!" The servant stopped and faced her mistress again. "Thank you for everything you do."

Kitty raised her eyebrows. Cassandra knew she was behaving strangely, and dismissed the maid with a wave of her hand. As soon as she heard the click of the door, she left the protection of the bed drapes and walked to the dresser. She poured cold water into the white porcelain basin and attempted to wash off as much soot as possible. She glanced in the mirror; her hair was a fright. Her teary eyes contrasted brightly with her ash-streaked face. A quick knock sent her scurrying toward the bed, and on her "Come in," two manservants entered carrying buckets of steaming water. They poured the water into the tub that stood before the fireplace. Kitty followed with more hot water and then added rose oil. Another young maid carried in a tray laden with coffee and fresh scones and placed it within reach of the tub and curtsied in the direction of the bed. With a curious glance at Cassie, the four servants left.

After stripping off her undergarments, Cassandra lowered her body into the fragrant bath water and sighed with contentment. As she luxuriated in the tub, Cassandra reflected on how different her life was from Alex's — from most people's. She thought about all the privileges she still enjoyed and vowed not to take them, or the people who made them possible, for granted.

In the stable, Alex finished shoeing the three new horses. Her minor altercation with Lady Cassandra had been quickly forgotten. She enjoyed hard labor. She liked the feel of blood pumping through her muscles and the sweat trickling between her breasts. Wiping her eyes on the sleeve of her old wool shirt, she led the last horse back to its stall.

"You're a real beauty," she whispered to the dapple-coated horse as she patted its neck. The rugged Percheron draft horse from France had been an extravagant purchase, but he would make life a lot easier come planting time. Alex laid her cheek against his warm, muscular neck and breathed in the odor of horse. Sometimes it was the best smell in the whole world. Until, of course, she could bury her nose into the sweet scent of a woman, she thought with a grin. The gentle horse turned his great brown eyes on the woman nuzzling his neck, and softly expelled air from his flaring nostrils. Alex patted him one more time, threw oats into his trough, and banked the fire.

Wondering briefly if Cassandra was still upset, Alex left the stables and walked to the kitchen of the main house. Her long-legged stride took her quickly over the snow-covered yard. She liked the sound of snow crunching beneath her boots. Her jacket was slung carelessly across her shoulders. The cold air easily penetrated the material of her shirt and made her skin tingle. Feeling the hairs on her arms and neck rise, Alex hurried into the warmth of the kitchen. The room was filled with the aroma of roasting venison.

Mrs. Simmons, "Cook" to most everyone, turned at the sound of Alex stamping the snow off her boots. "My dear," she exclaimed. "Why don' ye wear yer jack? Ye'll ketch yer death, and then where wud we be?"

Shrugging, Alex threw the jacket over a chair and strode over to the roaring fire to warm her hands. "It's a short trip across the stableyard," she answered, smiling.

"I'll fetch yer some water fer a washin'," Cook replied as she bustled about. "An' 'ow 'bout a nice cuppa?"

"Coffee would be wonderful, but I'll get the bath water. Can you keep the men out of the kitchen for a few minutes?"

In answer, Cook bolted the two doors leading into the kitchen. The manservants knew when the doors were locked that they were to stay out. It didn't happen often — most servants washed briefly in the privacy of their own rooms.

Alex dragged an old battered tub out from a dark corner and brought it before the fire. The dull metal glinted with a muted shine left over from better days. Alex poured boiling water into the tub, followed by icy cold water to bring the temperature to a tolerable level. Unselfconsciously she stripped and then submerged herself in the warm, unscented water. She sighed contentedly and then soaked a few minutes before grabbing a large bar of lanolin soap to vigorously scrub the dirt off her body.

Busily fixing tea, Mrs. Simmons kept glancing at Alex, trying not to be obvious, as if she never ceased to be amazed by Alex's muscular build, bulging biceps, and hard thighs that seemed incongruous with her large breasts and rounded hips. Carrying a large mug of unsweetened coffee, Cook approached the tub and smiled at Alex. The steam rose and misted Cook's face as she placed the mug within Alex's reach.

"I don' know 'ow ye take so many baths. It ain't healthy. The doc tol' me so, 'specially wid the cold air."

Alex laughed and blinked as soap ran into her eyes. "I can't go to bed with soot on me, now can I? Besides, would you want to sleep next to someone who smelled like a stable?"

Mrs. Simmons blushed. "If'en I was married, 'twould be a natural odor."

"Was your husband a groom?"

Cook flushed a deeper red. "I never 'ad a 'usband. 'Tis a nicety ter call me Mrs., that's all."

Alex was silent, sorry that she had caused Mrs. Simmons pain. The cook went back her preparations for the evening's dinner. Alex quickly finished rinsing and then, feeling like a magnificent sea creature, rose from the water. Cassandra liked to see her this way and would be disappointed that Alex had taken her bath in the kitchen. She dried in front of the fire without using a towel, then put on a set of her spare clothes while she was still damp. She unlocked the kitchen doors and began to scoop tub water into buckets to take outside.

"No, no!" Mrs. Simmons admonished. "I'll get one o' the menfolk ter do that. Ye go on now. Ye got a formal dinner ter dress fer."

"Thanks, Cook." Alex bounded out of the kitchen. She'd forgotten about Aunt Sophia's dinner party that night. Alex wasn't particularly looking forward to the affair, but she knew it would make both Cassandra and Aunt Sophia happy. Besides, she was curious about the two new women. When the two had moved to the neighborhood, Alex had worked for them a couple of times. However, she'd never seen them herself, but always dealt with the estate manager. Servants gossiped that one of them wore breeches and rode horses astride.

Bursting into their bedroom, Alex was breathing heavily from having run up the stairs. Cassandra turned in surprise. She was wearing only her chemise while she brushed out her damp hair. The sight took Alex's breath away.

"You are so beautiful." She rested her big hands on Cassie's soft shoulders and leaned down to kiss her neck. The faint smell of roses assailed her nostrils. Cassandra turned her head so that Alex kissed her mouth instead of her neck. Their tongues flickered. Cassie moaned softly.

Alex laughed. She was always pleased with the

way Cassie reacted to her. She ended their kiss and went to sit on the bed, patting the coverlet beside her. Cassandra wordlessly got up and joined her on the bed. They put their arms around each other and Cassie pushed Alex backward. She kissed Alex's cheeks, mouth, throat, and the soft indentation between her breasts. Her hands wrapped around Alex's buttocks, squeezing them firmly. Alex slid her hands under Cassandra's chemise, feeling the smoothness of her soft skin. As she began to lift the chemise off, someone suddenly rapped loudly on the door. Startled, the two women leapt up. Alex strode over to stand beside the writing desk while Lady Cassandra smoothed down her chemise and ran her fingers through her hair.

"Come in," Cassandra said, her voice trembling.

Aunt Sophia glided into the room, bringing with her the scent of lavender that clung to her clothes. She smiled slightly, a knowing smile that made Cassie redden. Alex picked up a quill pen from the desk. Sophia stopped at the foot of the huge bed.

"I just wanted to remind you two of the dinner tonight. Jennifer will be arriving from London to stay for a fortnight or so and I have invited our neighbors, the Lady Anneliese von Rothenberg and her companion, Miss Clarissa Worthington. I believe Lady von Rothenberg is a German baroness."

She moved to the armoire and began rifling through Lady Cassandra's many gowns. "I want you to look your best, Cassandra. You have a tendency lately to dress very casually. Perhaps this pale blue silk?"

"Of course, Aunt Sophia," Cassandra said as she

joined the older woman. "I was thinking more of my cream muslin with the red sash." She turned to Alex and winked, knowing Alex wasn't the least interested in such a topic of conversation.

"And you, Alex?" Aunt Sophia turned to her as she fidgeted awkwardly beside the writing desk. "What shall we do with you?"

Alex hated all this talk of clothes. What did it matter whether one chose the blue silk or the cream muslin? She still didn't realize that Aunt Sophia and Lady Cassandra liked to tease her. She played nervously with the quill.

"I can't wear those clothes," she stated, embarrassed.

"I have just the thing for you," Aunt Sophia answered. "Come with me. I'll send Kitty up for you, Cassandra."

She walked sedately out of the room, beckoning for Alex to follow. Nearing panic, Alex obliged. She shot Cassie an anguished look. Save me, it said, but she had already turned her attention back to her mirrored image.

Down the hall in Aunt Sophia's room, Alex fidgeted in the too-soft chair she sat in. Sophia was rummaging through her vast closet, mumbling to herself. With a cry of delight, she pulled forth a frothy pink concoction of lace flounces and heavy satin. It was unlike anything Alex had ever seen. She felt the blood drain from her face.

"What do you think?" Aunt Sophia asked as she fanned the old-fashioned dress across her bed. "It's a bit old, but it should fit you. You're such a big, healthy girl."

"You can't mean for me to wear that," Alex exclaimed in horror. She recoiled and gripped the arms of the chair.

"Oh, Alex, you can't attend a formal dinner party dressed in men's breeches. Why, we don't even know these women. What would they think?"

"I've heard that Lady von Rothenberg herself wears men's breeches on occasion." Alex was desperate. How could she get out of this situation without offending her benefactor?

Aunt Sophia hid a smile. "Servants' gossip. Nothing more. Yes, I think I will have Kitty press this for you."

Alex leapt out of the chair. "With all due respect, madam, I cannot and I will not wear that ... that ... thing. You will just have to excuse me tonight."

"Alex, my dear." Aunt Sophia laughed. "I would never ask you to do such a thing. I'm only having a bit of fun. Here, this is what I really have for you to wear."

From her closet Aunt Sophia withdrew a plain white cambric shirt, subtly embroidered with pale green along the cuffs and collar, and a dark green riding skirt made of broadcloth. From between the tissue paper in her chest of drawers she pulled out a plain cream-colored chemise of lamb's wool.

"Do you think these would do? I hope they fit. The seamstress could only guess at your size."

Alex expelled her breath. She smiled sheepishly as she took the clothes from Aunt Sophia. "Yes, they will be fine. I can wear my boots?"

"Of course. We wouldn't want you to be too

uncomfortable, would we? Go on now and show Cassandra."

Alex went to their bedroom, but the younger woman had already gone downstairs. Alex carefully placed her new clothes on the bed. It had been years since she'd worn anything but breeches. With a resigned sigh, Alex glanced one more time at the clothes and then left the bedroom to find Cassie.

Lady Cassandra was waiting for Alex in the grand parlor. As Alex entered, the strains of a minuet caught her ear. Cassandra was playing the pianoforte. The afternoon sun filtered through the sparkling windows to cast a golden glow about the woman whose fluid fingers moved over ivory keys. A simple strand of diamonds glittered at her throat. Alex stood silently. She loved to watch the concentration in Cassie's face. The music ended, and Lady Cassandra looked up to see Alex.

She motioned for Alex to join her on a brocade-covered couch. She sat carefully, letting the chintz material of her pale yellow gown settle softly around her. She arranged her cashmere shawl into warm folds around her shoulders. Alex sat beside her and crossed her long legs. She gave a quick, admiring glance at her shining new Hessian boots before she looked at the blonde beauty beside her.

Wrinkling her brow, Alex said, "That was a mean trick you and Aunt Sophia played. I was trying to think of a way to get out of the dinner without insulting your aunt."

Cassandra smiled. "It was entirely Aunt Sophia's idea, I assure you. I wish I could have seen your face when she showed you that horrid gown. It must be thirty years old."

Alex laughed. "It was awful. Anyway, my love, I must finish my chores this afternoon. Don't worry, I'll be ready for dinner at seven."

CHAPTER 13

All was in readiness for the evening. The dining room shone in the light of a hundred candles. The crystal and silver were polished to perfection, placed upon a snow-white damask tablecloth. Sophia's best china glowed, and in its pristine whiteness reflected the colors of hothouse blooms.

Sophia gave the room one more nod of approval. It had been so long since she'd seriously entertained that she was nervous. Not only was Jennifer here, but two new ladies were coming. She and Jennifer had long ago acknowledged their feelings for each other, and tonight she planned to ask Jennifer to live with her. These intermittent visits from London just weren't enough anymore. Her niece and Alex would not stay forever, and she didn't relish the idea of being alone once again. Seeing how happy the two young lovers were made Sophia yearn for her own happiness. She looked into the large gilt mirror and patted her carefully coifed hair. She wished she didn't have so much gray in it. Because Jennifer liked her in blue, Sophia had carefully chosen to wear a satin gown of periwinkle. It's modest train whispered behind her with every step.

Running her fingers along the back of a chair to check for dust, Sophia wondered about her new neighbors. She knew the baroness was younger than herself, but whether she came into her title through marriage or blood was a mystery. It was not that unusual for a noblewoman to have a female companion, but the word was that Miss Worthington was not a companion in the servant sense of the word. With one last glance about the room, she went to the kitchen to check with Mrs. Simmons on how dinner was progressing.

Upstairs, Cassandra and Alex were getting dressed. Every now and then one of them would make a flirtatious attempt to lure the other into the bed. It was harder this time for Alex to maintain control, and Cassandra didn't make it easier by flitting about the room in next to nothing. Alex distracted herself by straightening the waist of her new skirt. Her long legs felt naked underneath without the familiar feel of tight breeches. At least the shirt is loose and comfortable, she mumbled under her breath. She looked in the mirror and began dragging a brush through her thick chestnut-brown hair.

Cassandra approached from behind and peeked over Alex's wide shoulders. "I need you to lace up my gown," she said. "Unless you prefer I call Kitty."

Alex turned and caught her in a big hug. "I'll help you," she replied, fumbling with the lacings of the chemise, trying to undo what Cassie had already done.

She pulled out of Alex's grip. "Bad girl," she said as she playfully smacked Alex's hands. "What would Aunt Sophia and her guests say if we were late for the preliminaries? Now, do me a favor and ring for Kitty. She needs to fix my hair anyway."

With a mock frown Alex complied. It didn't take long before Kitty knocked on the door and entered without waiting for a reply. She flushed deep red when she saw Alex standing there. It was still hard for her to get used to the idea that she and Cassandra slept in the same room. Alex didn't blame her. She probably had a vague notion of the way things were, but it was more likely the impropriety of a servant and a lady sharing a room that shocked her.

She gave a quick curtsy. "Yes, milady?"

Cassandra gestured toward the apple-green satin gown lying on the bed. Its color complemented the green embroidery on Alex's shirt. "I need you to help me finish dressing." She looked at Alex with laughter in her eyes. "Alex was just leaving."

Alex went downstairs to join Aunt Sophia in

drawing room. They sipped Madeira, slightly too sweet for Alex's taste, and waited for Cassie and Jennifer.

Jennifer came downstairs first. Aunt Sophia rose and walked over to greet her friend. She took both of Jennifer's hands into her own and kissed her lightly on the lips. "I am so glad you could come."

Jennifer spoke with a cultured Boston accent that was not unpleasing. "It's so good to see you, Sophia. London is so dreary this time of year." She turned toward the couch. "Alex."

Adopting the fashionable mode of dress, Jennifer wore a deep lavender velvet gown tied with a black sash under her breasts. The short puffed sleeves and square neckline were edged with matching black lace. Her long white gloves were decorated with black embroidery on the back of the hand. She carried a lavender reticule and a richly decorated silk fan. Her shiny black hair was caught back in a snood of antique fillet, but small curls framed her face. Amethysts glittered in her ears.

"May I offer you something to drink?" Sophia asked, and nodded at the serving maid.

The maid brought over a tray of goblets. Jennifer chose red wine over Madeira. She sipped the wine, grimacing over its sweet flavor. Alex smiled. She knew of Jennifer's preference for stronger spirits such as whiskey. Choosing not to have a second drink, Alex shook her head as the maid approached.

At last Cassandra entered the drawing room. She looked beautiful, with her hair curled and a new ribbon laced through it. Her emerald necklace glittered, drawing Alex's attention to her throat. Alex automatically stood when she entered the room.

"You look very beautiful tonight, Lady Cassandra," Jennifer said. "Green is very becoming. And you, Alex. You look very dashing."

Alex glanced down and twitched the skirt nervously. "It's been many years since I've worn anything like this. Do you think it suitable for Lady von Rothenberg?"

Jennifer laughed heartily. "From what I've heard of the baroness, she will find it much too feminine. But at least you are tall enough to almost put her to shame. She is a giant, from what the servants tell me."

"Jennifer!" Aunt Sophia exclaimed. "Don't tell me you listen to servants' gossip?"

"And you don't, my dear?"

Cassandra broke into the conversation. "I am most curious about her friend, Miss Worthington. She is a writer like you, Jennifer. At least, that is what I have heard."

"She writes poetry, I believe," Aunt Sophia said.

"My goodness," Jennifer responded, "from the way we talk it appears we are all gossips. And what have you heard, Alex?"

Alex glanced at the maid holding the tray of drinks, who was finding it hard to remain composed. Alex gave her a wink and a smile. Suddenly, the maid caught Aunt Sophia's eye.

"You may go now, Lisbeth," Aunt Sophia said belatedly.

Lisbeth bobbed a curtsy and took her heavy tray out of the room. The butler came in at the same time to announce the two expected guests.

"The Baroness von Rothenberg and Miss Clarissa Worthington," he said in his nasal tone.

All four women turned toward the door. The baroness was indeed tall, surely towering over most men. She entered with the haughtiness of her German heritage, but smiled to reveal large white teeth. She was a veritable Valkyrie — big-boned, with large breasts whose cleavage was deepened by the corset she wore beneath a plain gown of midnight-blue velvet. The color was striking against her pale skin, and made the blue of her eyes more intense. Her thick, dark blonde hair was swept back into a chignon of curls and free of adornment. She too wore long white gloves, but these she stripped off as she strode confidently into the room. Her eyes flickered over Alex, and then twinkled with knowing amusement as she approached her hostess.

Aunt Sophia's diminutive frame seemed even smaller as the baroness loomed over her. Alex wondered if she felt overwhelmed, but Sophia kept her composure as she held out her own gloved hand. Instead of the expected handshake, the baroness lightly kissed the back of Aunt Sophia's hand.

"I am very pleased to finally meet you, Miss Stonehurst," the baroness said in an accent rich with rolling r's. "May I present my companion, Miss Clarissa Worthington."

Clarissa stepped forward and took Aunt Sophia's hand in turn. She was of medium height, with a pleasing figure draped in a diaphanous gown of pure white. Her ghostly white skin was covered in a fine powdering of freckles. Titian hair was left unfashionably loose, held off her face only by a diamond headband. Pale gray eyes framed by colorless lashes gave her a haunted look that was easily belied by her warm smile. Her exotic perfume was unfamiliar.

"Anneliese and I have been looking forward to this for many days now." She spoke with a city accent softened by country living.

"We are very happy to meet you at last," Aunt Sophia responded. "May I introduce my niece, Lady Cassandra Stonehurst; her friend, Alexandra Ferrars; and my friend from America, Miss Jennifer Adams. She has settled in London. And please, you must call me Sophia."

Greetings were exchanged all around. It was a few minutes before dinner would be served, and the baroness chose to talk with Alex. "You must be the woman I have heard much about. You do not enjoy the fashions of ladies?" Alex flushed and the baroness quickly added, "I am not fond of them either, but like you, I did not wish to offend. I had this gown made especially for tonight."

Alex felt immediately at ease with her. "Aunt Sophia would not have been offended."

"She is in some way your aunt too?" Lady von Rothenburg queried.

"Oh no, I only call her that out of respect. She would not let me use a more formal title."

"I too do not like titles among friends," the baroness replied. "We are friends, yes? You will call me Anneliese and I will call you Alexandra."

Cassandra joined them just then. "Oh no," she laughed. "You must call her Alex. No one has said Alexandra for many years."

"Alex it will be, then."

Alex was awed by the forceful presence of the

Baroness von Rothenberg. She had never met a woman like her. It was good to know other women could be strong. Instinct told her that the baroness had never been married. She looked around the room; none of them had been married. It proved what she had always known — that women didn't need men to survive. Indeed, they were better off without the male sex.

Her memories flashed back over her youth. She had slaved so hard in the fields trying to prove herself. She felt she had worked longer and more diligently than most of the men working beside her. As her strength grew, so too did her confidence. She had fought off any man who tried to get the better of her. Then she met Cassie, and there was the terrible incident with Lord Alfred. She shuddered. Of course, she couldn't forget the nightmare ride to save Cassandra from the brigands who surely would have raped her. She thought of all she had done on Aunt Sophia's estate, all without male guidance. She felt herself smiling broadly.

The baroness was still talking to Lady Cassandra. "... and you must come to tea the day after tomorrow. You and Alex. And tell her she must wear her breeches so I can wear mine."

The butler stepped into the room. "Dinner is served," he intoned.

The six women filed into the formal dining room, which was all aglow with candles and filled with the fragrant odor of roses and beeswax. It seemed only natural that Aunt Sophia would lead, placing her small hand on Jennifer's arm. Behind her walked Clarissa, who placed her hand in the crook of Anneliese's elbow. And lastly came Alex and Cassandra, who merely held hands and smiled into each other's eyes.

A few of the publications of
THE NAIAD PRESS, INC.
P.O. Box 10543 • Tallahassee, Florida 32302
Phone (904) 539-5965
Mail orders welcome. Please include 15% postage.

CRAZY FOR LOVING by Jaye Maiman. 320 pp. 2nd Robin Miller mystery. ISBN 1-56280-025-6		$9.95
STONEHURST by Barbara Johnson. 176 pp. Passionate regency romance. ISBN 1-56280-024-8		9.95
INTRODUCING AMANDA VALENTINE by Rose Beecham. 256 pp. An Amanda Valentine Mystery — 1st in a series. ISBN 1-56280-021-3		9.95
UNCERTAIN COMPANIONS by Robbi Sommers. 204 pp. Steamy, erotic novel. ISBN 1-56280-17-5		9.95
A TIGER'S HEART by Lauren W. Douglas. 240 pp. Fourth Caitlin Reece Mystery. ISBN 1-56280-018-3		9.95
PAPERBACK ROMANCE by Karin Kallmaker. 256 pp. A delicious romance. ISBN 1-56280-019-1		9.95
MORTON RIVER VALLEY by Lee Lynch. 304 pp. Lee Lynch at her best! ISBN 1-56280-016-7		9.95
LOVE, ZENA BETH by Diane Salvatore. 224 pp. The most talked about lesbian novel of the nineties! ISBN 1-56280-015-9		18.95
THE LAVENDER HOUSE MURDER by Nikki Baker. 224 pp. A Virginia Kelly Mystery. Second in a series. ISBN 1-56280-012-4		9.95
PASSION BAY by Jennifer Fulton. 224 pp. Passionate romance, virgin beaches, tropical skies. ISBN 1-56280-028-0		9.95
STICKS AND STONES by Jackie Calhoun. 208 pp. Contemporary lesbian lives and loves. ISBN 1-56280-020-5		9.95
DELIA IRONFOOT by Jeane Harris. 192 pp. Adventure for Delia and Beth in the Utah mountains. ISBN 1-56280-014-0		9.95
UNDER THE SOUTHERN CROSS by Claire McNab. 192 pp. Romantic nights Down Under. ISBN 1-56280-011-6		9.95
RIVERFINGER WOMEN by Elana Nachman/Dykewomon. 208 pp. Classic Lesbian/feminist novel. ISBN 1-56280-013-2		8.95
A CERTAIN DISCONTENT by Cleve Boutell. 240 pp. A unique coterie of women. ISBN 1-56280-009-4		9.95
GRASSY FLATS by Penny Hayes. 256 pp. Lesbian romance in the '30s. ISBN 1-56280-010-8		9.95

A SINGULAR SPY by Amanda K. Williams. 192 pp. 3rd spy novel featuring Lesbian agent Madison McGuire. ISBN 1-56280-008-6		8.95
THE END OF APRIL by Penny Sumner. 240 pp. A Victoria Cross Mystery. First in a series. ISBN 1-56280-007-8		8.95
A FLIGHT OF ANGELS by Sarah Aldridge. 240 pp. Romance set at the National Gallery of Art ISBN 1-56280-001-9		9.95
HOUSTON TOWN by Deborah Powell. 208 pp. A Hollis Carpenter mystery. Second in a series. ISBN 1-56280-006-X		8.95
KISS AND TELL by Robbi Sommers. 192 pp. Scorching stories by the author of *Pleasures*. ISBN 1-56280-005-1		9.95
STILL WATERS by Pat Welch. 208 pp. Second in the Helen Black mystery series. ISBN 0-941483-97-5		8.95
MURDER IS GERMANE by Karen Saum. 224 pp. The 2nd Brigid Donovan mystery. ISBN 0-941483-98-3		8.95
TO LOVE AGAIN by Evelyn Kennedy. 208 pp. Wildly romantic love story. ISBN 0-941483-85-1		9.95
IN THE GAME by Nikki Baker. 192 pp. A Virginia Kelly mystery. First in a series. ISBN 01-56280-004-3		8.95
AVALON by Mary Jane Jones. 256 pp. A Lesbian Arthurian romance. ISBN 0-941483-96-7		9.95
STRANDED by Camarin Grae. 320 pp. Entertaining, riveting adventure. ISBN 0-941483-99-1		9.95
THE DAUGHTERS OF ARTEMIS by Lauren Wright Douglas. 240 pp. Third Caitlin Reece mystery. ISBN 0-941483-95-9		8.95
CLEARWATER by Catherine Ennis. 176 pp. Romantic secrets of a small Louisiana town. ISBN 0-941483-65-7		8.95
THE HALLELUJAH MURDERS by Dorothy Tell. 176 pp. Second Poppy Dillworth mystery. ISBN 0-941483-88-6		8.95
ZETA BASE by Judith Alguire. 208 pp. Lesbian triangle on a future Earth. ISBN 0-941483-94-0		9.95
SECOND CHANCE by Jackie Calhoun. 256 pp. Contemporary Lesbian lives and loves. ISBN 0-941483-93-2		9.95
MURDER BY TRADITION by Katherine V. Forrest. 288 pp. A Kate Delafield Mystery. 4th in a series. ISBN 0-941483-89-4		18.95
BENEDICTION by Diane Salvatore. 272 pp. Striking, contemporary romantic novel. ISBN 0-941483-90-8		9.95
CALLING RAIN by Karen Marie Christa Minns. 240 pp. Spellbinding, erotic love story ISBN 0-941483-87-8		9.95
BLACK IRIS by Jeane Harris. 192 pp. Caroline's hidden past . . . ISBN 0-941483-68-1		8.95
TOUCHWOOD by Karin Kallmaker. 240 pp. Loving, May/December romance. ISBN 0-941483-76-2		8.95

BAYOU CITY SECRETS by Deborah Powell. 224 pp. A Hollis
Carpenter mystery. First in a series.   ISBN 0-941483-91-6   8.95
COP OUT by Claire McNab. 208 pp. 4th Det. Insp. Carol Ashton
mystery.   ISBN 0-941483-84-3   9.95
LODESTAR by Phyllis Horn. 224 pp. Romantic, fast-moving
adventure.   ISBN 0-941483-83-5   8.95
THE BEVERLY MALIBU by Katherine V. Forrest. 288 pp. A
Kate Delafield Mystery. 3rd in a series. (HC) ISBN 0-941483-47-9 16.95
                         Paperback   ISBN 0-941483-48-7   9.95
THAT OLD STUDEBAKER by Lee Lynch. 272 pp. Andy's affair
with Regina and her attachment to her beloved car.
                                          ISBN 0-941483-82-7   9.95
PASSION'S LEGACY by Lori Paige. 224 pp. Sarah is swept into
the arms of Augusta Pym in this delightful historical romance.
                                          ISBN 0-941483-81-9   8.95
THE PROVIDENCE FILE by Amanda Kyle Williams. 256 pp.
Second espionage thriller featuring lesbian agent Madison McGuire
                                          ISBN 0-941483-92-4   8.95
I LEFT MY HEART by Jaye Maiman. 320 pp. A Robin Miller
Mystery. First in a series.   ISBN 0-941483-72-X   9.95
THE PRICE OF SALT by Patricia Highsmith (writing as Claire
Morgan). 288 pp. Classic lesbian novel, first issued in 1952 . . .
acknowledged by its author under her own, very famous, name.
                                          ISBN 1-56280-003-5   8.95
SIDE BY SIDE by Isabel Miller. 256 pp. From beloved author of
Patience and Sarah.   ISBN 0-941483-77-0   9.95
SOUTHBOUND by Sheila Ortiz Taylor. 240 pp. Hilarious sequel
to *Faultline.*   ISBN 0-941483-78-9   8.95
STAYING POWER: LONG TERM LESBIAN COUPLES
by Susan E. Johnson. 352 pp. Joys of coupledom.
                                          ISBN 0-941-483-75-4   12.95
SLICK by Camarin Grae. 304 pp. Exotic, erotic adventure.
                                          ISBN 0-941483-74-6   9.95
NINTH LIFE by Lauren Wright Douglas. 256 pp. A Caitlin
Reece mystery. 2nd in a series.   ISBN 0-941483-50-9   8.95
PLAYERS by Robbi Sommers. 192 pp. Sizzling, erotic novel.
                                          ISBN 0-941483-73-8   8.95
MURDER AT RED ROOK RANCH by Dorothy Tell. 224 pp.
First Poppy Dillworth adventure.   ISBN 0-941483-80-0   8.95
LESBIAN SURVIVAL MANUAL by Rhonda Dicksion.
112 pp. Cartoons!   ISBN 0-941483-71-1   8.95
A ROOM FULL OF WOMEN by Elisabeth Nonas. 256 pp.
Contemporary Lesbian lives.   ISBN 0-941483-69-X   8.95

MURDER IS RELATIVE by Karen Saum. 256 pp. The first Brigid Donovan mystery.	ISBN 0-941483-70-3	8.95
PRIORITIES by Lynda Lyons 288 pp. Science fiction with a twist.	ISBN 0-941483-66-5	8.95
THEME FOR DIVERSE INSTRUMENTS by Jane Rule. 208 pp. Powerful romantic lesbian stories.	ISBN 0-941483-63-0	8.95
LESBIAN QUERIES by Hertz & Ertman. 112 pp. The questions you were too embarrassed to ask.	ISBN 0-941483-67-3	8.95
CLUB 12 by Amanda Kyle Williams. 288 pp. Espionage thriller featuring a lesbian agent!	ISBN 0-941483-64-9	8.95
DEATH DOWN UNDER by Claire McNab. 240 pp. 3rd Det. Insp. Carol Ashton mystery.	ISBN 0-941483-39-8	9.95
MONTANA FEATHERS by Penny Hayes. 256 pp. Vivian and Elizabeth find love in frontier Montana.	ISBN 0-941483-61-4	8.95
CHESAPEAKE PROJECT by Phyllis Horn. 304 pp. Jessie & Meredith in perilous adventure.	ISBN 0-941483-58-4	8.95
LIFESTYLES by Jackie Calhoun. 224 pp. Contemporary Lesbian lives and loves.	ISBN 0-941483-57-6	8.95
VIRAGO by Karen Marie Christa Minns. 208 pp. Darsen has chosen Ginny.	ISBN 0-941483-56-8	8.95
WILDERNESS TREK by Dorothy Tell. 192 pp. Six women on vacation learning "new" skills.	ISBN 0-941483-60-6	8.95
MURDER BY THE BOOK by Pat Welch. 256 pp. A Helen Black Mystery. First in a series.	ISBN 0-941483-59-2	8.95
BERRIGAN by Vicki P. McConnell. 176 pp. Youthful Lesbian — romantic, idealistic Berrigan.	ISBN 0-941483-55-X	8.95
LESBIANS IN GERMANY by Lillian Faderman & B. Eriksson. 128 pp. Fiction, poetry, essays.	ISBN 0-941483-62-2	8.95
THERE'S SOMETHING I'VE BEEN MEANING TO TELL YOU Ed. by Loralee MacPike. 288 pp. Gay men and lesbians coming out to their children.	ISBN 0-941483-44-4	9.95
	ISBN 0-941483-54-1	16.95
LIFTING BELLY by Gertrude Stein. Ed. by Rebecca Mark. 104 pp. Erotic poetry.	ISBN 0-941483-51-7	8.95
	ISBN 0-941483-53-3	14.95
ROSE PENSKI by Roz Perry. 192 pp. Adult lovers in a long-term relationship.	ISBN 0-941483-37-1	8.95
AFTER THE FIRE by Jane Rule. 256 pp. Warm, human novel by this incomparable author.	ISBN 0-941483-45-2	8.95
SUE SLATE, PRIVATE EYE by Lee Lynch. 176 pp. The gay folk of Peacock Alley are *all cats*.	ISBN 0-941483-52-5	8.95

CHRIS by Randy Salem. 224 pp. Golden oldie. Handsome Chris and her adventures.	ISBN 0-941483-42-8	8.95
THREE WOMEN by March Hastings. 232 pp. Golden oldie. A triangle among wealthy sophisticates.	ISBN 0-941483-43-6	8.95
RICE AND BEANS by Valeria Taylor. 232 pp. Love and romance on poverty row.	ISBN 0-941483-41-X	8.95
PLEASURES by Robbi Sommers. 204 pp. Unprecedented eroticism.	ISBN 0-941483-49-5	8.95
EDGEWISE by Camarin Grae. 372 pp. Spellbinding adventure.	ISBN 0-941483-19-3	9.95
FATAL REUNION by Claire McNab. 224 pp. 2nd Det. Inspec. Carol Ashton mystery.	ISBN 0-941483-40-1	8.95
KEEP TO ME STRANGER by Sarah Aldridge. 372 pp. Romance set in a department store dynasty.	ISBN 0-941483-38-X	9.95
HEARTSCAPE by Sue Gambill. 204 pp. American lesbian in Portugal.	ISBN 0-941483-33-9	8.95
IN THE BLOOD by Lauren Wright Douglas. 252 pp. Lesbian science fiction adventure fantasy	ISBN 0-941483-22-3	8.95
THE BEE'S KISS by Shirley Verel. 216 pp. Delicate, delicious romance.	ISBN 0-941483-36-3	8.95
RAGING MOTHER MOUNTAIN by Pat Emmerson. 264 pp. Furosa Firechild's adventures in Wonderland.	ISBN 0-941483-35-5	8.95
IN EVERY PORT by Karin Kallmaker. 228 pp. Jessica's sexy, adventuresome travels.	ISBN 0-941483-37-7	9.95
OF LOVE AND GLORY by Evelyn Kennedy. 192 pp. Exciting WWII romance.	ISBN 0-941483-32-0	8.95
CLICKING STONES by Nancy Tyler Glenn. 288 pp. Love transcending time.	ISBN 0-941483-31-2	9.95
SURVIVING SISTERS by Gail Pass. 252 pp. Powerful love story.	ISBN 0-941483-16-9	8.95
SOUTH OF THE LINE by Catherine Ennis. 216 pp. Civil War adventure.	ISBN 0-941483-29-0	8.95
WOMAN PLUS WOMAN by Dolores Klaich. 300 pp. Supurb Lesbian overview.	ISBN 0-941483-28-2	9.95

These are just a few of the many Naiad Press titles — we are the oldest and largest lesbian/feminist publishing company in the world. Please request a complete catalog. We offer personal service; we encourage and welcome direct mail orders from individuals who have limited access to bookstores carrying our publications.